STATIONS

Short Stories Inspired
by the
OVERGROUND LINE

Edited by
Cherry Potts

ARACHNE PRESS

This collection first published in UK 2012 by Arachne Press
100 Grierson Road, London SE23 1NX
www.arachnepress.com
Stations © 2012 Arachne Press
ISBN: 978-1-909208-01-8
Edited by Cherry Potts
The moral rights of the authors have been asserted
All content is copyright the respective authors.
For copyright on individual stories see page 3
Printed in the UK by TJ International, Padstow.

Many thanks to Muireann Grealy for all her help with proofreading this book, any remaining errors are mine. C.P.

CONTENTS

THE OVERGROUND

Introduction
Cherry Potts

The Overground runs at the bottom of my garden and my local station is a three minute walk away. Before there was the Overground, there was only Southern, but trains went to London Bridge, Victoria and Charing Cross. With the advent of the Overground, the Charing Cross trains were lost, and with them, the possibility of an easy last train home from many of my favourite central London venues. There was lamenting, there were protests, there was a coffin carried on the very last train. It was epic.

Then there was the disruption: the endless sleepless nights while the track was relaid and the station lengthened and the trees on either side of the cutting massacred. (More protests).
There were the huffy, *what use is it?* conversations on rush-hour platforms, the disbelieving sneer when told the value of my home would increase, followed by the overcrowding, the noise … and then there was the eating of words.

Because the Overground is wonderful. It cut ten minutes off my journey to work, it halved the time to get to all sorts of North London places I had given up going to: the King's Head, the Union Chapel and the Estorick Collection. It made getting to the Geffrye museum *simple*. It expanded my horizons. I ate my words.

Mentioning this in passing at a writing group meeting (spitting distance from an Overground station, average door to door journey eight minutes), as we settled for a twenty-minute writing exercise, Rosalind said: *we should write about the Overground.* So we did.

From that twenty minutes blossomed the idea for an entire book, with a story for every station on 'our' section of the line: Highbury & Islington to New Cross, Crystal Palace and West Croydon. Advertisements were placed, notice boards plastered, emails sent, and gradually over six months, the stories started coming in. The relevance of the trains themselves has faded into the storytelling a little, but the Overground remains the raison d'être of the book. So: thank you, Overground.

HIGHBURY & ISLINGTON

Inspector Bucket Takes the Train
Peter Cooper

It was a rare thing for Inspector Bucket to take the train, old fashioned as he was about travel and much preferring the jogging of a hackney cab or omnibus to the snorting of a steam train. He complained that the railway only showed him the backsides of warehouses and factories and what he wanted, he said, was the courts, alleyways and streets of London, for it was there that the pickpockets and thieves of London Town would ply or plan their trade.

Indeed, despite the unpleasantly windy weather, we had travelled all the way from Vauxhall to Highbury & Islington Railway Station in a hackney cab rather than risk the train. The Inspector had been asked to attend a meeting there, he said. Yet here we were: him at his advanced age and me his long-term amanuensis, due, after all, to catch an evening train from North London Railway's newest station.

It must be said that the station was a fine gothic building with an impressive forecourt, although its architecture was, frankly, more convivial than its railway staff! The clerk in the booking hall eyed us up as if he assumed we were only there with the intention of pinching the railway stock.

Mind you, I must confess I was embarrassed by Inspector Bucket talking loudly about an expensive gold necklace he said he had previously wrapped up in a handkerchief. He had been passing it from pocket to pocket rather obsessively. There was a niece of his in Kew who had been promised the jewellery as part of her wedding equipage, it seemed, but I saw no need for Inspector Bucket to announce this to the whole station. Also, now that we were exposed under the gas lights of the booking hall, I was alarmed at the state of his dress – particularly his greatcoat, which seemed very much a second best affair and rather stained at the pockets. Bucket had always been somewhat eccentric but now it seemed old age was making him careless.

Nevertheless, I was more surprised by the station itself than I was by the enigmatic Inspector Bucket. This was a busy and freshly appointed London station, yet it was strangely quiet and empty on what should have been a bustling Monday evening. I reasoned that it must have been the weather putting people off; though at the front of the station there was no pause in the movements of the cabs, the carts, the pedlars and the omnibuses. In the booking hall there was a small group of businessmen, a clergyman in a cassock and a rather handsome unaccompanied woman, but, apart from these, and a late-arriving gentleman who might have been an iron master from the manufactories, the booking office was doing slow business. A small number of other passengers were taking shelter in the first class waiting room and a few third class ones were leaning morosely against the glass, trying to find some shelter from the gale that was blowing up on the open platform. Several of the gas jets were already blown out and others were fitful. It was a relief to see the Cock Tavern, newly built into the station's eastern wing, where a passenger with a thirst on him might wait in more convivial surroundings in front of a fire.

We sat in the corner out of habit but just as I was about to quiz Bucket about tonight's exploits we were joined by an important looking gentleman.

'Inspector Bucket?' he said. 'I'm Beddows.' This was clearly the man whom Bucket had arranged to meet.

'I've a nephew who works on the railways,' Bucket said by

way of an answer. 'He's always trying to get me to take a ride on a steam locomotive, but it don't seem natural to me!'

I noticed the inky stains on Bucket's fingers but I thought little of that at the time, other than observing to myself that he must have been writing through the long hours of the afternoon and that his elderly carelessness extended to the ink bottle.

'Then, I'm very grateful to you for coming at all, Inspector,' the gentleman was saying. 'I wouldn't have asked you but we're desperate, you see. We're losing revenue because of it all and the police have been unable to do anything about it!'

Bucket had retired from the Police Force nearly twenty years before, to open his own private detective bureau, but he was still always addressed as Inspector.

'There are regular reports of robberies on the trains and we can't seem to do anything to prevent them,' Beddows continued wearily. 'Even as passengers sit in their carriages they're not safe! The result is that the station and the line are being by-passed by the better class of customer. Like you, Inspector, they'd sooner take a hackney cab, or omnibus,' he sighed despairingly. 'Most of the complaints from our passengers seem to mention the run from us to Willesden Junction. We're the new station so I've got the rest of the railway board on my back to get the culprits caught – and I'm at my wit's end, I don't mind admitting it!'

'And what precautions have been taken, Mr Beddows?' asked Bucket.

'Well, Inspector, the station masters have put warning notices on the platforms, of course, advising people to travel in groups if they can, and especially in the evenings,' said Beddows. 'Our ticket officers and guards keep a careful lookout for shifty looking characters and we've asked for policemen to be on patrol at all the station exits and entrances. We've even had our own men travelling in the carriages, ones sworn in as county constables I mean, but they can't keep a watch on every carriage, can they?'

'Would put off most thieves, I expect,' said Bucket thoughtfully, 'all those men in uniform. But I think you must have a local gang, and a brazen one, working your line – if the thefts are still occurring, that is?'

'Well, there has been a let-up in the complaints, but only, I think, because we've fewer passengers travelling; but that's not a solution the Board likes!' Beddows sighed, taking out his watch at the sound of an approaching train. 'That will be the seven o'clock coming in, Inspector. You'll journey on the line for us, won't you, and see what you think? I have a pass for you and your companion here.'

'No need, Mr Beddows,' smiled Bucket. 'I thought it more appropriate to purchase tickets of our own. Now, if you will excuse me, we have a train to catch.'

There was a small group around the first class carriages, most of them warily sizing up their fellow passengers even as they hastened to get out of the gale. However, instead of the usual desire to find a carriage of their own, they seemed more intent in finding safety in numbers. Bucket was again noisily informing me that I shouldn't concern myself and that the gold necklace was safe with him. He even patted gently at the very pocket. My concern at the signs of his growing confusion began to grow.

Our chosen carriage already had four people inside and the seats were narrow, but the blue buttoned cushions were comfortable enough. We were joined by a businessman, a young woman, and the clergyman. Only one of the gas jets was lit and this almost blew out before the door was closed by the manufacturing gentleman. When he sat down I felt that he seemed somewhat familiar but he paid no attention to me. Despite the cold outside, it seemed really quite warm in the carriage, squashed up with all these other people, and I noticed that even Bucket had unbuttoned his greatcoat.

Not a word was spoken by anyone other than the Inspector

and, for a while, he seemed never to stop: 'Won't cousin Ada be pleased with the gold necklace?' he was saying. 'It'll look fine on her, set off her other jewellery to perfection – though the gold necklace is far superior to anything cousin Ada has ever worn before, and she's worn pieces envied at many London balls and by many a London jeweller, ain't she?'

I felt embarrassed by his odd outpourings and looked out of the window at the dark shapes passing by. I am ashamed to say I was pretending that this old man in the later stages of his dotage had nothing to do with me.

No-one alighted until we reached Camden Town. A middle-aged lady carrying a small child was peering through the carriage windows as we pulled in. The clergyman took a good look at her, I noticed. When she finally settled on our carriage, the worthy manufacturing gentleman chose that moment, conveniently, to exit, or there would indeed have been a crush. She wore a heavy tweed cape, and the child was exceedingly well wrapped up in woollen blankets against the squall. She was a bustling, verbose personage who began addressing her fellow passengers from the first moment of her entry.

'I feel so much safer travelling in a full carriage,' she said. 'You hear so many stories, don't you? That poor gentleman who was murdered and left for dead on the tracks – do you remember reading about it? I know it was a few years ago, but, well, he made the mistake of sitting by himself, alone in a first class carriage, and nobody heard his screams, did they? Well, how could they, with all the noise of the engine and the train lines rattling? Hackney wasn't it? Where it happened, I mean. Well, I've been nervous about travelling on the railway ever since, haven't you?'

These observations seemed to give little comfort to her fellow passengers. The clergyman sitting next to me was looking nervous and the lady on the other side alarmed. The businessman clutched his case of papers more closely to his chest. I watched the gas jet flickering fitfully. The chattering lady continued to make similar comments almost all the way to the next station, only pausing when her little girl began moaning.

'There, there,' she said to her, and then looked up at us all. 'My niece has been unwell, you see, and I must get her back to her dear mummy. Would you mind awfully,' she said, addressing the clergyman who was sitting next to the window, 'if we were to open the window just for a moment? I think the child is rather warm.'

The clergyman complied with her request without saying a word. The window was opened, a gale blew in and the remaining gas jet blew out. We were plunged into darkness and confusion. There was a scream and some gasps, and then a sudden jostling in the carriage. Somebody stood up, I imagined to extinguish the gas, or perhaps to attempt to re-light it, and I felt a hand brush past mine where I was sitting next to the silent Inspector Bucket. If the intention was to re-light the gas, it was evidently unsuccessful; however, after a moment, the window was shut again and to everyone's relief we began to pull into the lit precincts of Chalk Farm Station. Everybody was back in their seats and glad to be in some light again, even smiling at each other in acknowledgement of our recent predicament and panic.

'Well, this is my stop,' said the lady, cradling the silent child in her arms.

'This is the termination for us all, I believe!' said Bucket suddenly, standing up. 'I must ask you all to step off the train for a moment.'

Everyone was aghast, not least myself.

'What's the game?' said the clergyman, whom I had not heard speak until that moment and who sounded less like a man of the cloth then any I had ever heard. 'Who do you think you are?'

'I'm no-one,' said Bucket, 'but this here gentleman is someone.' The manufacturing gentleman who had left our carriage earlier had obviously just stepped out on to the platform at Camden and then stepped straight back into the next door carriage. He was now waiting, sentinel-like at our door, holding out his badge of office. He was a policeman! And now I recognised him as none other than our old friend Sergeant Meehan (now an inspector) who had been involved in the case of The Beast with us. As soon as a pair of burly officers had joined him from their position at the station's exit, the passengers in the carriage had little choice but to step down.

'What's it all about Constable?' the middle-aged lady was saying. 'My poor daughter is ill you see. I must get her home.'

'Oh, 'daughter' is it this time?' said Bucket, raising his eyebrows. 'You'll be ashamed of yourself now, I expect, won't you – using this 'ere small child for cover! Where have you picked the poor thing up from, eh? The streets? Hold her still, Inspector Meehan. Let's see what we have hidden under these woollens, shall us?'

The small child whined but Bucket was gentle with her. 'We won't hurt you, my duck,' he said, and withdrew an ink-stained handkerchief wrapped around something shiny from amongst the folds of material. 'Well, what have we here?' he said, unfolding the handkerchief and holding its contents in his open, inky hand. 'Look, an expensive gold necklace! Now, how did she come to have that tucked under her blanket, I wonder?'

In Bucket's hand was not a necklace, of course, but a glass eye-dropper as used by doctors. A small amount of ink, or, as I discovered later, aniline dye, was still in the bottom of the unstoppered bottle.

'I think we shall find a few ink stains on you too, madam,' he said. 'Shine your light here, Constable.' And indeed there were stains, all down the woman's dress and on the cape she was wrapped up in.

'And your conscience will be stained too I expect, Vicar,' said Bucket, staring at the clergyman. The light was duly shone and revealed a cassock stained with purple dye.

'You picked my pocket when the light went out and you passed the parcel to this lady here, who then hid it under the child's blanket,' Bucket explained. 'But I took the stopper out of the bottle just as you was dipping it out and the ink has shown who did it! Well,' Bucket said, nodding at the constables to apply their handcuffs, 'my friend at Highbury & Islington will be very pleased to have you two off his line while you walk up and down another one, doing shot drill at Tothill or Newgate. Take them away, Mr Meehan.'

'Well,' I said, when the figures had disappeared into the shadows, 'You've surprised me again, Inspector Bucket. Is it back home on the next train then?'

'No, my boy,' he said, 'call us a cab.'

HIGHBURY & ISLINGTON

Morning, Sunshine
Louise Swingler

'Mornin' darlin'!' he says, 'Ah, you're an angel. You bring me a little bit of sunshine, you do.'

He takes the polystyrene cup from me, and places it carefully on the pavement. He's sitting with his bottom half still tucked into his dirty red sleeping bag, and I can see the gloss of the earlier rain on the shiny fabric. I drop a pound in the old margarine carton on the grubby green blanket in front of him. The blanket flaps at the edges in the chilly March breeze.

'Thanks darlin' — you're too good to me, you are.'

'Ah, no,' I say, feeling as I always do that his sweetness deserves more than the small round coin I give him whenever he's here. But it adds up to about twenty-five pounds a month, what I spend on him. Money's tight, with our impossible mortgage, but at least we've got the house that goes with an impossible mortgage, so I shut my ears to the cash-till in my brain. I don't always feel like a sandwich at lunch anyway. I'm a bit early for work, so I light a fag, and offer him one.

'I don't mind if I do,' he says, flashing a gappy but still charming smile from under his brown, unwashed fringe. He can only be about thirty, possibly younger. He has small sores on his pale skin, around his mouth and one on his neck; I can see it above the washed-out collar of the faded black rugby shirt he often wears. The sleeping bag isn't one of those plump ones that taper towards your feet; this looks more like it cost a fiver at

Argos – thin and flat, with a zip that's buckled and broken half-way down. It must leave his flank exposed to the wind.

'D'you like my display?' he says, squinting up at me. Today he's drawn some pictures, which are laid out across the blanket. One is a thousand smudges of green, blue and brown – a river coursing through green mountains. I wonder where he got the crayons; they look like quite good quality. On the blanket there's also one of those red and yellow plastic windmills on a stick – you see them at the seaside in the top of sandcastles – but this one's stuck in an old beer bottle, and now he picks it up to blow it. He has to blow hard, because one of the sails is a bit bent. He looks like a kid, his lips pursed up, a little spittle going with his breath into the windmill. I laugh, and he pauses, looking up with a half-smile.

'It's lovely,' I say.

'Ah, you've got to put on a display,' he says, winking and pushing the fag I gave him behind his ear, 'I like to make gorgeous ladies like you smile.'

And he does cheer me up; every day. More than anyone, actually. His *morning, darlin'*; or *morning, sunshine*, depending on how grey the day is, makes a difference.

Every morning, when I dash out of Highbury & Islington Station, I queue for a coffee from the silver trailer outside the station. Then, as I wait to cross Holloway Road at the pedestrian lights, I peep through the fast-flowing traffic to see if the giant scarlet caterpillar is lying alongside the wall of the bank opposite. If I can't see it, I feel a little pang of disappointment as I hurry across the road. If he's there, I give the coffee to him. If he's not, I drink it when I get to the office.

I wave goodbye to him as I set off along the path across Highbury Fields, to the large mansion house where I work. Heights-Mitchell Developments, half way up on the opposite side, looking out in self-satisfied splendour over the fields.

'Hey, I'm making another surprise for you,' he calls,

'make sure you come back later.'

About half-past five, we parade past him at speed on our way down to Cheriton's. Peterson has booked their conference room for the monthly board meeting, and afterwards there'll be wine and canapés in a sectioned-off part of the restaurant. Peterson strides along with Nigel, our Finance Director, and Fiona and I struggle to keep up, carrying plastic bags packed with agendas and papers. I can only grimace at sleeping-bag-man, and I try to point at my watch to show I'll be back later. He sends me a little salute, and rests back against the brick wall.

As we dash down Upper Street, I think of my girls waiting at Auntie Gee's for Stu to collect them; it's the second time this week he's had to do it, and he was pissed off. Your job's too much, he says. But it's me that's too much. The part of me that enjoys the way it grips me like a vice. *I need some figures for a meeting tomorrow, Jen. But it's five-thirty already, Mr Peterson. I know, Jen; is there any way you could stay a bit late? Oh, okay, then, just this once.* That's how it goes, and I feel a little thrill when he leans on my desk, looking harassed and stressed out, and another when I give my agreement and he smiles with relief. It's all a game; we both know I'd never refuse, but it's a good game. He really rates my work; makes me know that I'm essential. Stu makes me feel crap at everything; a shit mother who's never there; a wife who can't keep house. I make a mental note to swipe some of the posh finger food to take home for the girls.

It's an important meeting tonight. There are two representatives from the Residents Association in the area where the next Heights-Mitchell project is to be built. Peterson's strategy is to make the deputation feel listened to, and to impress them with our corporate responsibility projects over a few glasses of free wine. But I've seen this pair at a consultation meeting, and although they look a bit grey and rubbed out at the edges, you can tell they've been lobbying for one thing or another ever since the 1960s. Nothing gets past them; they're like crows at lambing time, picking your eyes out if you don't keep moving. But that's not completely fair; they do seem to act from a bedrock of integrity. Tested against Vietnam. Honed at Greenham. It's Class A activism, not nimbyism, and I think Peterson's too young to really get that. He's only about twenty-eight, although he looks older since his promotion. He's lost weight and the skin around his eye sockets has gone a bit pouchy, but his black hair is still glossy and thick.

They're already there when we arrive. Grantly Witherthwaite and Pet Nanceworth. Grantly looks as mild and inoffensive as his name. He's wearing a charcoal-coloured anorak which has one of those fastenings that demurely hides the buttons from view. He wears crisp old-man jeans, and has a well-clipped, speckled beard. Pet is tall and terribly thin, her face lined and tanned by a thousand fags, her tight, shoulder-length curls dyed a tinny red colour. She's wearing black leggings and a purple tunic with a slash-neck which shows up her deeply-ridged clavicle bones and her scraggy throat. God, she looks tense; as if she could explode like a light bulb into silvery egg-shell fragments.

I see Pet's thin lips compress even more tightly as her gaze settles on Tanya Selton. When Tanya came back from the last negotiation meeting with the Residents Association, she was swearing blue murder about these two. Peterson doesn't usually allow representatives at Board Meetings, but he thinks they'll be mollified if they're allowed closer to the 'seat of power' as he calls it. Honestly! Even I have to admit he can sound a bit up himself sometimes. We're a building development company, not the White House. But it's just his way of talking himself up enough for the battle; he needs this to go well. It's the first big project with him at the helm and he's determined it's going to be cutting edge, which, of course, is half the problem. Too modern for the residents.

Grantly sits up straight and coughs drily before setting out his points to the tableful of well-dressed board members.

They're all displaying the sort of concerned, thoughtful look that I'm sure must be taught on Day One of whatever training courses politicians attend. Grantly's tone is slightly judicial and didactic. It reminds me of last night, when Stu and I had one of our meandering 'discussions,' where he tries to cajole me into to going part-time and I resist. He thinks he'd get on more quickly if I did; he's aiming to be Area Manager within a year. He says his pay-rise would compensate for losing half my wages, and he recites an endless list of additional benefits. How can I explain my refusal when the main reason I want to hold onto this job is in case I can't stand it anymore and need to leave him? So I just keep letting him needle me, and it's exhausting. Now Peterson turns and winks at me as he prepares to speak, and I feel a gush of pleasure.

After Peterson has answered Grantly's points, Pet takes over, her voice getting squeakier and her pomegranate-coloured curls shaking as she repeatedly stands up and is asked to sit again. She declares that Tanya has ignored, has *concealed*, evidence about the dangerous condition of the ground under the site. Tanya shakes her geometrically-bobbed head with a supercilious smile on her lips that is even annoying me; can't she play the game and be pleasant? Peterson is rattled too, and he's trying to get her eye, but Tanya just smiles down at her mauve nails. She manages to look so classy, despite the lacy black bra showing through her blouse, and those outrageous long talons. But then Pet leaps up again and strides towards Tanya, who momentarily cowers as she sees Pet's wiry arm raised, the bony hand in a fist – God, No! Peterson is on his feet and around the table already, one of his arms held out stiffly across Tanya's brocaded bosom, the other hand forming a fan to cover her face. Peterson braces himself as the angular bones of Pet's bare forearm collide with his suited one; he has to use some strength to withhold the blow. Pet rubs her arm and cries out 'But she's a bloody liar', and Peterson's voice sounds almost liturgical as he booms 'Sit down now, Mrs Nanceworth. Please go and sit down.' And she does. No-one else has moved. No-one else needed to.

After the drinks session, Fiona and I stay to finish the half empty bottles. We are still high on the energy that near-violence spawns, and we have already relived the moment when Peterson's arm shot out in front of Tanya about fifty times. It was a great moment – despite all his young-man's *brouhaha*, I saw his basic goodness concentrated in his posture, in the undeniable nobility of his protective act. And it ended in victory for Heights-Mitchell. After Pet was asked to leave, it was obvious that Grantly was shocked and ashamed, so a compromise was quickly reached.

Later, Fiona and I stumble drunkenly back along Upper Street, and now we're hooting with laughter as the unintentional comedy of the evening takes hold of us. The slightly righteous seriousness of Peterson's rigid arm, stuck right out, and Pet bouncing off it like a cartoon character running into a wall. We have to keep stopping, we're laughing so much.

'Oh don't get the poxy train,' Fiona says, as I turn in behind the Post Office which conceals the entrance to Highbury & Islington Station, 'come and get a cab.'

It's cold now, and I'd love to wander up to the yellow-fronted cab office with her. She would get out at Archway and give me a fiver, and then I'd take it the rest of the way over Highgate and down to Child's Hill. But I've hardly any cash on me, and if I get any out now Stu will see my overspend when he checks the accounts. Bloody internet banking; it leaves nowhere to hide.

'No, I'll catch the ten past ten,' I say.

As Fiona walks on up to the cab office, she turns and assumes Peterson's now legendary stance, with her arm out and that daft look on her face, making me giggle as I run into the station.

It's empty on the westbound platform. I look over at the other platform, where the North London Line trains used to stop, before they made this into a four-platform station. Sinful people like me used to congregate at the far end there, skulking against the wall to smoke a furtive fag. Can't get away with that nowadays, either. There's so little leeway left. Nine minutes to go. I shiver a little, and think of Stu getting angrier with every extra second that passes. I find tears climbing out of my eyes as I imagine what it must have felt like, being protected by Peterson's arm, but I squash that thought. Self-pity only makes you weak, and anyway, Stu would never hit me. I'll just have to out-bluff him over this part-time business. What was it my favourite vagrant said this morning? You've just got to put on a display for people.

Oh, shit! Sleeping-bag-man – I said I'd go back. He probably saw me walk past with Fiona, shrieking and larking about like he didn't exist. Still eight minutes to go. If I miss this one the next one isn't for twenty minutes, but I think I could make it, at least to say goodnight and slip him a fag.

I charge up the steps, passing through the cloud of balmy, tropical air that hangs at the end of the ticket hall where the escalators come up from the Underground. Outside, the chrome coffee van has long gone, and a few rough-looking lads stand outside the Cock drinking lager from bottles. As I cross the road I see that the red caterpillar has already zipped himself up for the night, and I slow down, wondering whether to run back to the station, but I see something odd – is it a black bin-liner or something? No, it's moving. It's a bloke in a donkey jacket, squatting down and poking at the sleeping bag. I can hear his voice raised in disgust; *come out of there, you waster ... come out before I drag you out...* I walk briskly across the pavement, and I see Peterson's strong, straight arm in my mind's eye, and I shove my own arm between this ugly, fat bloke and the inert body lying on the cold ground.

'Fuck off,' I yell, 'leave him alone! Just go and – get lost.'

I laugh, because I nearly said 'go and sit down,' like Peterson said to Pet. The man pushes up from his crouch, and he's shocked when he sees me properly; a smallish forty-something woman in a tight skirt and short business jacket. But then he smacks out at the air, and there's a hollow pop like a ball hitting a coconut, and I hear a dreadful noise like a donkey in pain, and it's seconds before I realise it's the noise of my own lungs, trying to suck in the air he's knocked out of me by chucking me against the wall. I topple down next to sleeping-bag-man and roll onto my side. I put my hand to the back of my head where I find a miraculously huge egg growing on my skull. I push my face into the red fabric – why isn't sleeping-bag-man waking up to help me? Oh, yes, I'm supposed to be helping him, aren't I?

'Come on; leave it,' a man's voice says, 'that old fella's calling the cops.'

I roll over and see an elderly man in a neat, charcoal anorak talking into his phone, standing over by the road. Oh, fuck, it's Grantly. 'No, don't,' I murmur, 'Not the police'. This'll be the final piece of ammunition for Stu. I pull myself up but I feel dizzy and nearly fall, and my hand pushes down on the red sleeping bag. It's soft – too soft. It seems I have successfully defended a load of old clothes and smelly blankets.

I rush past Grantly and across the road. I'm back in the station, and the beeping that indicates the train doors are shutting has already begun as my heels clatter on the metal edges of the steps down to the platform. I jump into the first carriage just as the doors shudder to a close. I sit down and grab a Metro off the seat, opening it so that it hides my face from the few other passengers. I try and focus on the newsprint, but it shimmers like a mass of oily, black spaghetti. I wait until the letters regain their distinct shapes and my breathing is in synch with the soothing rhythm of the train. I put the newspaper down and sit looking out. The train embraces each dark station in turn, its doors emitting a swish of a kiss as they open to the longing of the empty platforms. And I will be on the train that travels back and greets each one of them again tomorrow. Good Morning. Good Morning. Good Morning.

CANONBURY

All Change at Canonbury
Paula Read

Luke definitely felt something when the well-known actor slipped his hand lightly across the front of Luke's comfortable khaki twill trousers. The twills were Luke's Sunday slacks, a pair he favoured most especially for weekend wear, even though on this particular Sunday, he was at work in his surgery.

But what was it he had felt exactly? He couldn't find the word. Puzzlement made creases appear in his broad forehead, downy and pale beneath the grey/blonde tongue of fine hair that lay across it.

'Hey Luke, I can call you Luke, can't I?'

Luke nodded, the actor continued.

'Hey Luke, why are you looking so sad, man?'

'Um. Not sad, not sad. This is my worried expression,' stuttered Luke. How could he tell this beautiful young American man that he suspected him of making a move on him while lying on the orthopaedic bed, naked, receiving the touch of Luke's expert hands. And anyway, why would such a young man – Luke emphasised the 'young' – even be interested in him, already fifty-five years old with excitement an unusual event in his life.

Ah, that was the word – excitement. He felt excited. The actor had put his head down again, waiting for Luke to resume the manipulation of his sore muscles. When the session was over – a lucrative one for Luke, an emergency call out of the usual hours – Luke waited for the young man to dress. They shook hands in the outer office.

'That was great, Luke. Thanks. I'll come again next Sunday. Same time?'

'Yes, yes, of course. Very happy. Happy.' And Luke made himself busy with the laptop. But the actor didn't leave. He stood in front of Luke, until Luke was forced to look up from his bureau and into the hazel eyes of the actor, flecked with more green than brown. Full of – what? The actor's expression was unreadable. He held Luke's eyes for some seconds. Then turned and loped towards the door, one hand reaching forwards to open it, the other tucked into his jeans pocket.

'So long. Until next week.'

He turned at the door, saluted and was gone – striding down the street. Luke watched him go. That look. Luke felt it again, the excitement. As he packed up the surgery, tidying up an already immaculate room, Luke's thoughts turned to Kate. She would be at home, preparing lunch, chatting to Humphrey, the Labrador, who would be sniffing around her feet, hoovering up crumbs.

Luke locked up. His surgery was on the ground floor of a tall apartment block, built of traditional greyish yellow London brick around the turn of the nineteenth century. It had been a lucky find twenty years ago when Luke had set up his practice, not outrageously expensive, before Islington had developed its present cachet from rubbing shoulders with prime ministers and their acolytes. With the Canonbury Overground station nearby, Luke was sitting on a comfortable spot of property, something that gave him quiet satisfaction.

Luke's building overlooked a small communal garden, enclosed in wrought iron railings, typical of this North London neighbourhood. It was spring. The trees were just coming into leaf. The birds were wild with activity, calling to each other urgently from treetops. On an impulse, Luke pushed open the gate and went into the garden. He felt a sudden rush of joy. Here he was, sap rising all around, sap rising in him. He relived the hour he had just spent, easing the knottiness in the young actor's muscles, laying his hands on the twists and coils, the trapezius and the deltoids, the iliac crest and the laterals, the lower gluteals, the perfect bottom. As Luke felt the warm skin beneath his hands again, imagined the glorious golden back with its slightly prominent vertebrae, something stirred. Luke flexed his hands, curling and uncurling his long fingers. He stood up abruptly from the old wooden bench where he had sat gingerly, eyeing the lichen, thinking of his khaki twills. Oh Lord. What was that in his trousers? He hadn't seen that for a while. He lowered himself again, pulled on his light-weight Burberry, stood, smoothed himself down – Kate, Kate would be waiting.

The next Sunday, the actor arrived early. Luke was at his laptop, ostensibly organising his next week's appointments. His heart was fluttering. The actor appeared in the doorway at the very moment Luke had actually focused on his screen for a split second. The actor's body stopped the streaming sun suddenly. Luke noticed the absence of light, threw up his head awkwardly. Good heavens. He would need an osteopath himself. And there he was: the beautiful young man. Luke's heart was throwing itself around his chest.

'Hey man, how ya doing?' The actor saluted him. Luke cleared his throat. They shook hands vigorously.

*

On his way home that evening through the balmy air of mid-May, shirtsleeves pushed up uncharacteristically, his jacket looped over a finger and slung over his back, Luke was in ecstasy. The initial brush across his trousers had been translated into the most ardent sexual encounter Luke had ever experienced. Once again, he stepped into the communal garden across from his building, found a bench and sat down to relive the past hour, the most intense of his life. He shifted a little, embarrassed, as if others might read in his face the sheer luxury and pleasure of what he had just been through. What had surprised him was his own lack of self-consciousness when the actor had run his smooth square hands over his body, introducing him to a world he had never known but that was, nevertheless, totally familiar.

Luke took the Overground at Canonbury with the Sunday travellers out for the day, politer than the daily commuters, jostling each other amiably, talking to their children rather than to their phones. For once, Luke wasn't irritated by the jostles and slowness of the Sunday riders. He was in no hurry to get home to the large, airy flat in Docklands that he shared with Kate. This was odd, because they both looked forward to Sunday lunch at their rosewood dining table, an heirloom from a long-dead grandmother, in the window alcove overlooking the river. Whatever the weather, the river entertained them. They would eat companionably, something delicious prepared by Kate, watching the river.

The flat was an odd choice for Luke, whose natural tastes led to the classic brick buildings of the old world, even though he had spent a nervous adolescence encased in such a building. Kate, of course, had talked him into it. Luke was surprised to find his fish out of water feeling soon evaporated and he would saunter, yes saunter, up to the smart block, admiring the clean square lines of the building, the light glittering on the many glass surfaces. What would he do without Kate, without her ability to imagine a different kind of life?

'Luke, darling, where have you been? This is not a meal that can wait around. Quick, wash your hands, set the table. I need to serve up.'

Luke stopped fussing with Humphrey, patting his broad back as he went to do as he was told. The sweet scent of roast garlic followed him down the hall to the vast bathroom, tiled in black and white and gleaming with polished chrome.

Here, he was able to wash away the scent of the actor which still clung to his body, reluctantly. A thrill ran through him. A delicious, hungry thrill.

'So, who is this client you have to see on a Sunday, Luke? That makes two Sundays in a row. You aren't normally so keen to give up your weekends.'

'Um. He's American. Actor. Appearing at the Old Vic I think. Quite well-known. Films.'

'Oooh. You have to let me meet him. Handsome, is he?' Kate giggled; her round, apple-cheeked face creasing up, her blue forget-me-not eyes disappearing into the pale flesh.

'Mmm. Very handsome.' And Luke tried not to look dreamy, busying himself with laying the table with the silver service left to him by his mother, who died still begging Luke not to leave her, her strong fingers coiled like wire around his wrist.

Kate chattered as they ate, about Humphrey's toilet habits – he enjoyed taking a very public crap along the river walk, always ignoring the discretion of the bushes that lined the walk – about the tales told by the children in her primary school - the nine free-flying budgies in one small flat, the time Uncle so-and-so thumped the Staffie cross breed so hard it died, why Mum wasn't home at night on account of her job. And Luke responded as he always did, smiling, nodding, as always impressed by Kate's affability and compassion.

Outside their third floor window, the river gleamed. Luke cleared the dishes as he always did, then announced he was going for a stroll. Kate looked at him quizzically. This was not Luke's usual habit.

Please don't come with me, Luke begged silently.

'Do you want company?' Kate smiled at him, but all Luke could think was how much he didn't want to be looking into the faded features of Kate's fifty-three-year-old face, but into the warm brown-green eyes of his lover.

*

Magical Canonbury. Magical Sundays. Magical love. For that's what it was. Luke was engulfed. And then – this.

The Old Vic run was ending. The play and the actors would be transferring to New York. It was midsummer when Luke learned the news. The two of them were relaxing late into the Sunday afternoon in a brasserie on Upper Street. There was no show that night. Kate was out with friends. Only Humphrey would miss Luke.

They touched their feet together discreetly under the table. Luke didn't dare to hold hands in case a client saw him.

'I love you Luke, you know that,' said the actor, 'but I have to go. This is my life we're talking about. Acting is all I've ever wanted to do.'

Luke couldn't breathe. How could he go back to the life before? He had slowly unfurled like a new leaf, giving himself to something he had never dreamed of. And now that dream was ending. Luke realised he would not be able to lead a life of casual sex, grabbed here and there, while parading his conventional life with Kate in front of the small world of friends they had created together.

When they parted, just after the actor had delivered this bombshell, there was no 'So long. Until next week.' There was no kiss goodbye. There was nothing. Just an empty space.

Luke crossed the road, holding back the sobs that were threatening to explode from his throat. He found the Canonbury garden, found his bench, sat with his head in his hands as the tears dripped through his fingers. All, all was gone now. He had been awakened and now the dead hand of inevitability was lying across his bent back, forcing Luke to suck back the tears, straighten himself up, tidy his clothes, climb back into his pupa, become again Luke, of Luke and Kate, Canonbury osteopath and East London primary school teacher. The comfortable couple. He thought suddenly of his mother, dead now for ten years. Not a day went by when he didn't experience a moment of dread that she might actually still be alive. He knew exactly what look would be in her blue gimlet eyes. Scorn.

It was darkening now. How long had he been sitting there? Canonbury Overground was busy, Sunday travellers milling. Luke made his way through them, not seeing anyone.

'Oy, watch it mate,' a bald man yelled, as Luke's shoulder was wrenched back by contact with the other man's. Luke shook his head, focused on the fast-moving mouth of the bald man, mumbled an apology, went on through the crowd.

But what if – what if Luke followed him, followed his lover, left everything behind, took a chance, breathed again? The dead hand on his back started to shift. Luke unbent in his narrow train seat; sat more upright, faced the people opposite as the train rushed him back to his life. Why not? Why not? Why not?

*

Luke let himself in quietly. It was late. Kate might be asleep. Time to talk tomorrow. Time to –

The light went on abruptly in the alcove of the main room. Kate was sitting in the upright chair, upholstered in green-brown cotton velvet. She had a glass of wine in her hand. As Luke approached, Kate stood up. She set down the wine, patted down the jersey trousers she always wore around the house and announced:

'Luke, I'm leaving you. She's called Lana.'

DALSTON JUNCTION

Moving Mike
Wendy Gill

'Dalston? Where's that Mike?'

'The flat's really great, Mum, you'll love it, I know you will ...'

Dalston? That's east London I recall, biting my lip in consternation as his words continue to pile down the phone, clambering for an exit.

'It's like a penthouse – on the eighth floor, wrap-around balcony – great views over London and it's got a concierge and a gym ...'

Perched on a stool, coffee, now cold, in one hand, phone in the other, right leg almost swinging off its knee; there's a fog in my head. He's only just left student digs in Brighton and moved in with his girlfriend, Jenner, who has a good job and a lovely first floor flat in one of those Regency houses in Hove, close to the sea. I know there's been tension between them; Mike a creative, writing music since he was twelve; Jenner a grounded businesswoman, five years his senior.

Discarding the coffee, I slump onto the breakfast bar, elbows as props. My dumbfounded reflection stares back from the polished kitchen window, facing the garden. I watch a robin frisking in the birdbath. Paranoia sets in – Mike must be high on something, maybe he's a drug runner or dealer. I stall for time: 'My goodness, Mike, sounds like a real bachelor pad.'

'It's brand new, Mum – four bedrooms – there'll be four

of us sharing the place; me, Adam, Rob and Tristan. The rent's not bad between four of us, all the others earn good money. I'm sure I can get a job, even if it is only bar or restaurant work to begin with ...'

My leg slows to a metronomic lilt.

'What about Jenner, Mike?'

'We're taking time out from each other. She's already given notice – doesn't want to stay on in Hove on her own. Says she wants to move back to London anyway, better for her career. We've got to move out in two weeks' time. D'you think you could give me a hand? Oh, and the flat in Dalston isn't quite ready yet, they're still building it – the agent reckons it'll be about six weeks – just the floors to put down. Is it alright if I move in for a month or so?'

*

I drop Mike's sister, Amy, at school and set off for Hove. Traffic on the M25 is moving. Through the windscreen a sky of trivial blue, fanned by corpuscular rays, sheds a diffuse light on my foreboding. The plan is to empty Mike's chattels into my car by lunchtime, have a bite to eat, Jenner's at work, but she may join us, and be back in North London for school turning out time for Amy. No pressure then. I asked Mike to be ready. He assured me he didn't have much to move. It'll all fit into the car, no problem, he said.

But Mike's never been ready.

An image of his primary school teacher pixelates in my mind; arms folded so tight as to perform the duty of a Wonderbra, shoulders hunched high enough to pop a blade, and a frown to match. Her words play out in my head – *Now then, Michael; he's very clever, but so laid back as to be quite horizontal. To be honest with you, he frustrates me so much I don't know what to do with him.* I moved him to a Prep school; less aggressive, but the same message – *Don't worry, Mrs Martin, some boys take a long time to get kick-started, my son didn't get going until he was twenty-two.*

I discussed it with my mother, sadly no longer with us – *Mike's a darling, he's one of life's dreamers, and the world needs its dreamers; he'll be fine, don't worry,* she said. Right, Mum. She always was besotted with Mike and his ethereal blue eyes.

Notwithstanding certain glitches along the way, Mike now has a diploma in fine art, and a degree in sound art and digital music; possibly not the best spring-board to a financially secure future. He left our then comfortable family home, in Finchley, five years ago, when he was eighteen. Essentially, he was put out by his father, unable to deal with an artistic, teenage son – rather like one puts the dog out at night, except that Mike wasn't invited back in.

I left soon after.

A dark BMW cuts sharply in front of me. I realise I've been hogging the middle lane. In a demonstration of motorway etiquette, it indicates left and pulls into the nearside lane. Quite helpful, I think, just as the M23 exit sign comes into sight, which I may well have missed, until I spot a lone finger on the raised left hand of the anonymous driver. No need for that.

I accelerate and exit the M25.

The hands-free mobile rings. It's Mike.

'Hey, Mum. How you doing? Where are you?' his voice straining to start the day.

'Just joined the M23, be with you in about an hour depending upon traffic.'

'Great. I'll get some coffee on.'

'Mike –'

Silence. I can only speculate; poor reception, or his avoidance of my predictable inquisition.

Arriving at Hove, I squeeze my car into a space on Cambridge Road outside the flat. Mike buzzes me in. Climbing the stairs I see his lithe body slouched against a half open door. Only Calvin Klein boxers defend his modesty. He covers a yawn, removing his hand to reveal a heart-melting smile. We hug hello.

'Are you ready then, Mike?'

'Coffee, Mum?' he asks, pouring hot water into a cafetiere. I half nod, scanning the room for evidence of the imminent move. There's a pile of boxes stacked in one corner. Stepping closer, I see Jenner's neat labels depicting the contents of each box; summer skirts, sandals, court shoes.

'Have you packed anything, Mike?'

'It won't take long, Mum.' He reads my concern. 'I don't have much stuff.'

My eyes focus on the Clavinova; a full-size, electronic piano on legs. I bought it for him when he was just four years old: he learned to play it before he could read or write.

'Do you have a screwdriver, Mike?' He looks at me, face crumpled with incomprehension.

'The Clavinova. We'll never get it into the car with its legs on.'

The next couple of hours are fraught; fetching and carrying things up and down to the car. Nothing pre-packed. Jenner phones to see how we are getting on and to check where to meet us for lunch.

By now I've half emptied and re-packed the car several times over, at the kerb side; trying hard not to baulk at some of Mike's more dubious possessions. A couple of lads wearing Superdry t-shirts and low slung, crutch-at-the-knee jeans, risk losing them completely as they jump over the eclectic mound of items obstructing the pavement.

'Sorry, guys.' They smile back at me.

Resting against the car, eyes closed, I practise Pilates breathing. The deep in-breath fetches moist salty air, breathing out open-mouthed; the taste is on my tongue. I look downhill, out to sea. A mother and twin buggy approach. Attacking the pile, I struggle to make a wide enough thoroughfare. The woman pushes on through as if driving a snow plough; a front wheel gets stuck on the edge of a mirrored light-box advertising

STELLA ARTOIS. I move to help her, then cower, coughing, mouth full of smoke from the cigarette dangling from her left hand; with a defiant shove she crunches the S of ARTOIS.

'Silly cow,' she says, as if ready to spit. Her children cry in unison. 'And you two can shut up,' she yells, casting the butt of her cigarette back at me. She crosses the street some ten yards ahead.

I watch her diminish.

Mike appears with more belongings.

'Shit.'

'Sorry, Mike.' I collect up the shards of mirrored glass. But his stare is empty.

'Oh, never mind. No. It's just I've remembered, I left some stuff at my mate Tim's place – but it's on the way to the restaurant – can we stop off and pick it up please?' I tweak my lips into a transient smile. 'Thanks so much, Mum. I could never have done this without you.'

Eventually, we drive off, Clavinova upended through the sun-roof.

*

Mike stayed at Adam's place last night, so I'm taking the train. We're meeting at Dalston Junction, a station on the old East London line, well out of my comfort zone.

I dreamt Dalston last night – nightmare. The cast of Eastenders appeared, re-enacting the notorious murder of a three-year-old boy, bludgeoned and suffocated by his mother, which actually took place in the toilets at Dalston Junction in 1899. I've got Dalston sussed: intimidating, overcrowded; grimy, Victorian station; Mike's penthouse, an estate agents' hyperbole for an under-sized builders' yard.

Garbed in clothes usually reserved for dog-walking and armed with M&S anti-bac gel, I take the Tube to Highbury & Islington, then switch to the Overground. Waiting on the platform, my right eye starts to twitch; I hold the lid down, casting a cyclopic glance to see if anyone is watching. A train arrives which appears to be new, beige with orange livery. The carriage is surprisingly clean, half-empty. No squinting through dirty windows to read station signs, or fighting my way through malodorous armpits. A man sitting opposite, wearing a dark full-length overcoat and pointed shoes, looks at me, indifferent, as he rubs his nose. Several passengers are using their iPhones. The train slows again, stopping at Dalston Junction. Getting up, I feel scruffy and self-conscious, just missing a batch of the Big Issue to accessorise. Taking the stairs with the orange handrail to the station concourse, I grapple for my mobile to call Mike. Then I see him, waiting by the exit having a smoke. He discards the remainder of his roll-up.

'Hey, Mum,' we kiss, hello. 'You okay?' he asks, appraising me.

'I can't believe this, Mike. It all looks so new.'

'Didn't I tell you, this whole area is being regenerated? The station *is* new – well, re-built – the original dates back to eighteen hundred and something: I googled it.'

'That much, I knew.'

'Sorry, Mum, don't know about you, but I'm starving – didn't have time to eat at Adam's. Do you mind if we eat first? There's some great restaurants round here, and I need to send some emails, I might have a record deal.' I hold out my right arm.

'Lead on Macduff.'

Turning left from the station, I follow Mike into Kingsland Road, the main drag through Dalston. The buildings are old, some have seen better days, but the street is vibrant. We drop in at an internet cafe. The walls are bare brick, uneven; ceiling unfinished, floor raw concrete, furniture reclaimed. I order two juices of the day, carrot, ginger and apple, from a hirsute man behind the counter, and reach for my purse.

'It's okay, you pay later,' he says, in a soft, undistinguishable accent. 'Sit please, I bring to you.'

Mike is entranced, emailing.

At a table, two young mothers chat over their toddlers'

puréed food; one child sits mouth open, eager for another spoonful, his mother mid-sentence. A memory floods in – Mike, several months old, excited by a slimy grey pulp, his favourite, mashed banana. The other child, wearing a red velvet dress and patent shoes, runs to a low-level table where two professionals recline on faded leather sofas, lap-tops open. The little girl reaches in; she wants to press the buttons. One of them offers up her keyboard. The child giggles, excited. Her mother looks over, unperturbed.

On Mike's recommendation, we eat at a Turkish café, ordering Meze and Menemen. It's busy. Exotic spices deliver their aromatic message: awakening enzymes, inducing an intestinal growl. I blush. A waitress, moving deftly between the tables, places a kaleidoscopic platter before us. 'Is everything okay, madam? Would you like some water?' Mike smiles his appreciation. He tells me that in the London riots, Turkish shop owners were a major force in protecting Dalston.

Back on the High Street, I pause at the Art Deco cinema, its film listing fringe, cosmopolitan.

'Come on, Mum. I want to show you the flat – it's not far from here.'

We zigzag through crowded pavements, a myriad of sandwich boards and hats; black knitted, Rastas with red, gold and green stripes, skull caps, even the occasional fez. Mike always wears a hat; today's is a flat tweed cap. He dips left, looking back to check I am still behind him. A vivid mural covers the end of a building. It's gaudy, a carnival of people playing big brass instruments, rallying.

Across the road cranes hover, looking down upon the growing fashionable apartment blocks like proud parents surveying their offspring. Mike looks at me, eyes bright: 'This is it, Mum.' He steers me through the front entrance. 'The concierge isn't in post yet,' he explains.

We take the lift to the eighth floor, walk along a Travelodgestyle corridor until we reach the farthest oak-veneered door: opened by Mike's friend, Adam. They give me a guided tour. I joke about the likely state of the bathroom after the four of them move in. There's an open-plan kitchen-diner-living-room with full-height windows on three sides and the infamous wrap around balcony. The view over London is commanding: due south the Gherkin, iridescent in the fullness of the day.

Back at street level, Mike takes the opportunity to light up.

'Well, what d'you think, Mum?'

'I think it's great. I love this mural, Do you happen to know …' But I see something else: 'Dalston Eastern Curve Garden?'

'Let's go in, Mum – Andy might be there.'

Entering through a gate in a high wooden fence, I feel like Lucy stepping through the wardrobe. Instead of snow-covered Narnia, a haven of green, surrounded by tall buildings, hidden away like a precious gem, herb gardens and hand-made scarecrows, an oasis of calm in the midst of urban chaos. 'Andy?' I ask, pulling myself back to the conversation.

'He runs one of the local nightclubs. You wouldn't recognise this place after dark, Mum – you don't *see* Dalston, you *hear* it.'

In that moment I understand exactly what has drawn Mike to Dalston.

I know he's done his homework, this time.

HAGGERSTON

Platform Zero
Michael Trimmer

'Missed a good few spots there, Ems.'

Emily grasped the window wiper more tightly and knelt back down onto the platform's cold concrete, her eyes tracing the vague direction of where she thought her supervisor had meant. Nodding with false acceptance, she splattered the glass with the few remaining dregs of the cleaning fluid and began wiping again to finish a job she was sure was already done. With every stroke and re-clean, she reminded herself of the very good reason why she wasn't quitting.

She pulled the spray bottle's trigger again, this time hearing nothing but a struggling squeak. She shook it to show it was empty. Fran nodded and gestured for her to go get a new one from the platform's storage room.

Even if cleaning up after Haggerston Station's commuters was twice as bad as Emily thought, she still had to see it through. The last thing she wanted was a black mark on her employment history as the too-posh-to-wash-the-windows snob that couldn't hack it in the real world. She hadn't done four years of English Literature, two more of Comparative Literary Studies, and then spent the same time again contextualising every last chunk of meaning on gender conflict in Tolstoy all for nothing. If she could tough it out here, she could tough it out anywhere, something that would hopefully shine through on her CV when that shiny place in publishing made itself known.

Emily walked up to the far end that faced out onto the canal bridge. Despite being more protected here, surrounded on two sides by thick grey railing pipes, she still felt vulnerable, standing only a few feet away from the maintenance steps leading down towards the signal light box and the rails.

She pulled hard on the storage room door, using all her strength to stop it swinging through and denting the adjacent wall. They were serious about this room's security. Some of the spare parts for the ride-on sweepers and buffers they'd use down in the concourse cost nearly a grand. Even the walls round on the inside were plated in metal, to stop thieves just smashing their way in. She tugged the string of light switch. With a metallic click the bulb flickered on, sending the steel casing humming. The scent of settled dust, yesterday's rubbish bags, and shelf upon shelf of cleaning fluid hit her square in the nostrils. She looked over at the small hill of transparent rubbish sacks. Those would need taking out later.

As she reached for a new bottle from the appropriate shelf, darkness engulfed the room. Not just 'blown bulb' or 'dead battery' darkness. The purest, thickest, darkness Emily had ever known. She shivered as the few outlines she could very dimly see seemed to twist and split, as if her brain was processing the viewpoints of two sets of eyes observing the same scene.

Seconds later everything snapped back into focus, darker again. She reached to steady herself against the wall. She couldn't touch it. She couldn't sense resistance or feel anything. Nothing, nothing at all. Not even the ground beneath her feet.

The world spun. A noise like the whine of a thousand outdated modems screeched at her from every direction. She felt the instinct to screw her face up and cover her ears, but was unsure if she was actually doing it. The noise grew louder. She thought she felt herself stagger and trip. Her mind told her she was falling. Faster and faster, further and further. Further than she'd ever thought possible, even in her most ... her eyes opened. She was on the floor, still in the storage room, safe. But something was wrong. It was quiet. Too quiet. She stood up and opened the door.

All the other cleaners had vanished. There was no-one there. Thanks to budget cuts, there had only been two or three others before, but now, there was no-one. It was silent. Silent like she'd never heard. Other things were missing too.

There was no wind, no cars. No noise from anything nearby. She couldn't even hear the humming of the strip bulb. She walked back in and tapped it. It sounded different, like it was a solid block of glass. It still glowed, but was losing none of its energy to vibration. She pulled the cord to turn it off. It didn't respond. There was no click, no give. It didn't even feel like the same light.

She decided to head back down to the concourse, where the fuse box was housed. If she couldn't turn the lights off from there, something was very wrong. The more she looked around, the more she saw it. The station seemed – less detailed. The brickwork edging wasn't as sharp. Yellow lines at the platform edge were less textured. Signs proclaiming the station's name were blurry. Glancing round, noticing these flaws, Emily saw that there was a much bigger one outside the station.

She looked at the apartments, the lamp posts, the skyline in the distance, everything beyond the station's edge. She squinted, moved her head, walked up and down the platform. It was all the same. From every angle, as though somehow they'd become a projection or a painting. As she started to take this in, another blast of noise stuck home.

'Kraaaa! Kraaaa! Kraaaa!' It was like a klaxon, but spoken. 'Kraa! Kraa!' It wasn't like the screeching noise. This had a specific source, somewhere above the station. 'Kraa!' An eerie blue glow began shining from behind the other platform. She peered out. 'Dol!' A spoken word, but from a language she didn't recognise.

A whooshing noise was followed by a rush of air. She looked out for a second or two more, before her heart leapt up into her throat.

A gun. She only saw the barrel for a second before it disappeared behind the wall. Even from twenty yards away, having only seen an inch or two at most, she was sure of what it was. Moments later, she could just about make out half a dozen or so figures moving across the platform, picked out in the blue light.

Who were they? Why were they here? Where had they come from? They couldn't have come through the main entrance. The security guard would have stopped them, and even if he hadn't, she would have heard them, just like she would have heard them if they'd somehow abseiled down from the buildings beside the station, or used grappling ropes to climb up onto the bridge and ran along the rails. She knew all of these things were absurd, but they were much less absurd than the idea of them just appearing out of nowhere.

More noises. Clicks. Snaps. Cracks. Harsh, sharp and rhythmic, like someone throwing a string of polished stones. She backed into the storage room. Her foot sunk into a bucket filled with dirty water and three long mops. They fell forward, clattering against the metal wall. A sickly grey torrent flowed out the open door, onto the platform. She cried out with the pain of the ankle's awkward angle as she fell.

The clicks stopped. Emily held her tongue, suppressing the pain, shimmying backwards. She wished she could turn off the light, and did her best to angle herself out of immediate line of sight.

The clicks came again, slower this time. She could see the thoroughly unrecognisable shadow moving across the floor. Whoever it was, they seemed to carrying four or five poles that were moving in time with the clicks. That, at least, was what she told herself because she didn't think she could deal with the reality. A reality that made itself very clear when it rounded the corner and stared at her.

It had six legs. It backed away slightly upon seeing her. She would have done the same, if she wasn't already up against a wall. Standing about five feet tall and two feet wide, its 'torso' hung down between all its 'knees', complete with something like a head, and four smaller arms extending from just below that. Using two of these, it held its weapon, a long, thin looking thing, like a futuristic Lee Enfield. It wore what looked like armour on its legs and body, painted the same blue shade as the light.

It lowered its gun, then dropped it, and paced forward slowly. Moving two of its legs further apart, it swung its torso forward. It proffered a single, tentacle-like finger, plated in exoskeleton. Her mind processed this as a gesture of friendship, but the rest of her was still frozen with fear.

Just as she thought the creature had understood, a dazzling flash of red light struck it from behind. Scarlet sparks ensnared it, inducing something like a fit. Seconds later, it dropped to the floor. Emily looked through the door, and could see another, this time in red armour. It skittered away, either disinterested, or unaware of her presence.

For a moment, she lay still, looking at the creature's body. It was moving very slightly, and there was some noise too. Three short hisses, one after the other, and then a slight moan. It could have been breathing, assuming it needed to breathe. Taking a deep breath of her own, she stood up and skirted round it, careful not to trip on any of its limbs, and moved back towards the door to see what was happening outside.

There were two more of the creatures in red armour, firing towards the other platform. They seemed to be aiming in the direction of the blue glow, where something was returning fire. Despite the battle, the station looked intact. There were no bullet holes, burn marks or blast craters.

She pushed the door further round to get a better view

but it swung away from her, and smashed into the wall. The two red creatures rounded sharply at the noise. One of them was struck with an errant blue flash. The other redirected its attention towards her. She startled, frozen to the spot for a second, before darting back inside.

It had definitely seen her, she heard it getting closer. After what it did to the blue one… She shook, looking for anything she could use to defend herself. She saw the mops, the bleach sprays, the gun…

The gun! She looked at it. It was the only thing the creature might understand, but she couldn't… The noise of its footsteps got closer. She gulped and reached towards the blue's seemingly unconscious body, pulling the weapon out from underneath it. It was lighter than she expected, but still very cumbersome. Clearly, it wasn't intended to be held by someone with limbs anything like hers. She wrapped her fingers around two trigger-like-things either side of the barrel. They had some give, but she didn't want to pull too far. It was impossible to use one hand, so she propped the 'butt' of the weapon up against her chest. She breathed shallowly, trying not to cause too much movement in her chest, lest she set the thing off prematurely.

The thing moved into view. She twitched, raising the gun slightly. It didn't seem to be watching her. It held another object in its other two hands; a small rectangular box that looked as though it had a screen.

Sensing things were calmer, Emily lowered the gun. This had the unintended effect of placing it in the creature's line of sight for the first time. It skittered backwards, startled. She jumped, pulling the gun back against her body, spewing blue bolts of light everywhere.

The creature ran out of the room. Emily looked around. It had dropped a tiny black sphere on the floor. She looked at the thing, moving in closer. She heard a sustained hissing and could feel herself getting drowsier and drowsier. A sleeping gas? She couldn't believe such a thing could work so quickly. She had just enough time to prop herself up before she lost consciousness.

*

'We must apologise.'

Emily woke. Feeling dizzy, she sat up slowly and looked round. The room was large, white, brightly lit and almost entirely featureless. The only noticeable object was the bed she was lying on, which seemed to somehow rise seamlessly out of the floor. The voice came again.

'Your creation was not intended.'

Genderless, Received Pronunciation English. She looked up at the source. A human silhouette, solid black, projected into the air. It floated down towards her.

'We were creating a combat practice simulation arena. Your planet was one of thousands we take samples from. Your mass transit facility, a single scenario, one of billions we scan and recreate.'

'Scenario?'

'We run a scan of an area and recreate it to practice combat in that environment. We take samples from all across the galaxy. Agriculture bio-domes, radioactive waste silos, orbital shipyards, Zero-G military compounds, forestry enclosures, deserts, retail parks. We scan them and recreate them for practice.'

The meaning of the words filtered through slowly 'recreate?'

'A molecular replica. Atom by atom. Our machines create near-exact duplicates of – everything there.' Near exact, not the same. That explained why the light was suddenly solid and silent, why the text on the signs was blurry, why the brickwork hadn't seemed right. She began to understand.

'*I'm* a copy?' the thought struck her to her core. The strange blackness, the sensation of falling, the noise. That was how she processed having her consciousness duplicated, stored as a data stream, and then put together, quark by quark, atom by atom, from scratch.

'We did not intend to make you.' The figure explained 'Our bio-scanners detected the other life signs and filtered them out of the recreation. You were concealed in a thickly shielded area.' The storage room, plated with thick metal.

'Are you planning to invade?'

'Earth?' the figure replied. 'No. Earth contains nothing we value. We recreate it only for training.'

'I see.'

'We regret to inform you that, as you are a replica, your lifespan will be,' the figure paused, 'significantly reduced.'

Even with the voice's calm precision, Emily could hear subtle glimmers of emotion.

'How long?'

'Sixteen months.' That was all? She could feel herself trembling.

'We cannot send you back, nor can we heal you, but we are prepared to repay you in any way possible.' Repay her? What she really wanted was to go back home, but that wouldn't work. The real Emily would still be there, and she probably wouldn't enjoy being replaced for sixteen months, not unless she found a nice publishing job –

'You can recreate anything?' she asked, 'Anything at all, from the atom up?'

'Anything.' the figure replied, 'You may have anything you desire. We could design, for you, a paradise.'

'Can you make it more accurate, if you have to?'

'Yes. It can be exact. The scenarios are just for training.'

'Can you also put anything anywhere?' She asked 'Like the way you just appeared in the station, out of nowhere?'

'The teleporter.' The figure answered. 'You cannot go back though. If we were to be discovered –'

'No, not me.' Emily interrupted. 'It's for her, the real –' she struggled to say it, but powered through. 'You can make me a paradise later. There's something I need to send to Earth for *her* first.'

'A gift?' The figure asked. 'We can make, for her, anything at all.'

'What she wants, you can't make.' Emily answered 'But – you can make something that will let her get it, and put it in the right place.'

'We understand.' The figure replied 'What did you have in mind?'

*

To: emily.jane.gold@inbox.co.uk
From: sandra.meath@polluxpress.com
RE: Great Thesis! Let's talk!
Dear Emily,
This morning, on my desk, I found a leather-bound copy of your thesis on Gender Conflict in Tolstoy, with your CV tucked between the pages, and a post-it note stuck to the top saying 'read this!'

My staff all swear blind that none of them left it there. I don't know why, because whoever did put it there, I'm glad they did! I found you applied for our internship this summer, but with work of this quality, we'll need you much sooner and on a more permanent basis.

My secretary will be calling you later this week to arrange a meeting. Thanks again for sneaking this one in! I'm really looking forward to meeting you.
Yours sincerely
Sandra Meath,
CEO Pollux Press

HOXTON

Bloody Marys and a Bowl of Pho
Caroline Hardman

The sign was printed in elegant copperplate script on a piece of old parchment. Its once-black ink had faded in the sun and the tape sticking it to the window was yellow and peeling.

Closed for refurbishment. Opening November 2010

Norbert pressed his pale forehead against the window, the glass strangely warm against his skin, and tried to ignore the blank space where his reflection might have been. It had already been quite a traumatic morning; this was the very last thing he needed.

The problems had begun the moment he'd left his home in Brighton. To begin with he had boarded the train expecting to arrive at London Bridge, not Victoria. He had no idea how to get to the Kingsland Viaduct from Victoria, which meant having to ask for help. And that meant talking to other people which was, as a general rule, something Norbert preferred not to do.

No-one he asked had been able to help him anyway; several people had insisted on sending him to Dalston, where he certainly didn't want to go; a woman had tried to sell him some oysters and every time he turned around there seemed to be someone else thrusting a free newspaper in his face. He'd collected fourteen of the blasted things before he realised everyone else was saying no.

Even once he'd found an alternative route to Hoxton – one

that didn't need the Viaduct, which seemed to have disappeared completely, according to any of the maps he looked at – it had hardly been a comfortable journey. The first train he caught was cramped and crowded; he'd been leaned against, trodden on, glared at and elbowed out of the way more times than he could count. The next train was crowded too and to make matters worse when it arrived at Hoxton the station looked completely different. It had been most unsettling. Norbert couldn't understand why anyone would replace a perfectly functional train station or, for that matter, an entire train line with a new one.

And now this. He peered into the dark, deserted shop with its empty shelves and abandoned display case and felt tears prickle his eyelids. The one thought which had brought him some comfort as he negotiated the new-fangled ticket barriers and finally managed to leave the station was that he'd soon be exactly where he was now. Except, of course, he'd rather hoped to be standing on the other side of the glass.

Norbert had been coming to Hoxton Street Monster Supplies for as long as he could remember. The shop specialised in the kinds of products which would be impossible, or at the very least a little awkward, to procure anywhere else. It had first opened its doors in 1818 – Norbert's first visit had been not long afterwards – and had been supplying its grateful customers with magical spells, human-based food products and more practical items like fur conditioner and fang floss ever since. Although he rarely bumped into anyone he knew there, apart from Lucinda who sometimes worked behind the counter, Norbert always felt like he was among friends when he visited the shop. There was an unspoken code among the customers which meant that no-one minded who you were, or what you were buying.

He visited less often now than he once used to. Mainly because of the crowds; one trip to London every twenty to thirty years was as much as he could cope with these days. Norbert had always liked the fact that no matter how much the rest of the world changed between his visits, the shop remained steadfastly the same. There was something comfortably familiar about the ancient wooden shelves which creaked and groaned under the weight of their glass jars; he hoped the refurbishment wouldn't be too extensive. He looked at the sign again and wondered if any of the locals might know how long it had been there.

'Pardon me,' he said to a man in slim trousers and a baggy cardigan as he walked past. The man kept on walking, his head nodding subtly in time to a silent beat, and Norbert frowned. A group of young people were approaching and he tried again.

'Pardon me,' he began. 'Could you tell me how long this establishment has been closed?'

'This place?' one of the young men replied. 'I don't think it's ever been open.' A chorus of agreement came from his companions.

'Of course it's been open,' Norbert snapped. 'I've been coming here since…' he paused. 'For quite some time.'

The young man raised his hands and took a step backwards. 'Easy, mate,' he said. 'When were you last here?'

Norbert thought for a moment.

'1986' he replied, and the young man shrugged.

'You see? That's before my time. I was born in '87'.

Before Norbert could reply, a second young man, also part of the group, spoke to him. 'Those are nice threads, man. Where did you pick them up?'

Norbert looked down at his three-piece suit. It was already a little rumpled from his journey, but even full of creases it was far smarter than young man's outfit. His striped, long-sleeved t-shirt looked more to Norbert like it should have been underwear, and the hat he was wearing was rather unfashionable.

Norbert removed his own hat. Just because the young man had shunned the rules of etiquette he saw no reason to sink to the same level.

'Since you ask, this suit was made by my mother – she

was an excellent seamstress. The shoes are from Ardingers, and I bought this shirt some time ago; I'm afraid I can't recall exactly where. Jermyn Street, most probably, there's a tailor there I often use. James St Claire is his name.'

The young man's eyes grew wide. 'That shirt's an original James St Claire?' He turned to one of the girls. 'You're the fashion expert, Suzie. Is this guy for real?'

The girl stared at Norbert for several minutes. 'He's telling the truth,' she eventually said, and Norbert felt irritated. Of course he was telling the truth.

The girl continued.

'The collar's the right shape. And just look at the stitching.' Norbert grimaced as she poked unceremoniously at his shirt.

'Are you okay?' she asked him. 'You feel quite – cold. Like you're getting sick or something.'

'I'm fine, thank you.' Norbert said tightly. He wished his mother hadn't been quite such a stickler for manners.

The young man was still shaking his head in disbelief. 'Genuine James St Claire. How much did that set you back?'

Norbert stiffened. 'I'm afraid I can't recall' he said. It wasn't entirely true, but he was hardly about to enter into a conversation about money.

The girl who had been prodding him had turned her attention to the sign in the shop window. 'It says here they'll be re-opening in a couple of months,' she said. 'Can't you come back then?'

'I live in Brighton,' Norbert said curtly. 'It's not entirely convenient. And I've had quite a difficult morning already.'

'I see,' the girl said, with a sympathetic smile. She glanced at the others. 'Look, we're just on our way to the pub. Come with us if you like. A drink might warm you up a bit, at least?'

Norbert looked at the girl. She was a small, delicate thing, her dark eyes sunken and half hidden by her fringe. Her skin was almost as pale as his own and as she raised her chin a fraction she revealed an elegant, slim neck. Despite his mood, Norbert's mouth stretched into a long, thin smile.

'Thank you,' he heard himself say. 'After the morning I've had, a drink is exactly what I need.'

Almost as soon as they began to walk down Hoxton Street, Norbert regretted his decision. Once introductions had been made the young people had begun to talk among themselves and Norbert felt a sad, familiar feeling creep through his bones. It had been a ridiculous idea to join them. He was wondering whether it would better to silently slip away when they arrived at a building with bright lights above the door.

He felt a little better once they were inside. The room was large and pleasingly dark with deep green walls, thick wooden floorboards and a high ceiling decorated with red pressed tin. If not for the strange art on the walls and the cluttered bar running across the back wall, it could have been Norbert's own living room.

'What's everyone having?' asked the one called Cameron, once they had seated themselves around a low table in a corner of the room. 'Joel?' The other young man had slumped at the table, his head in his hands. He still had his hat on, Norbert noticed, and frowned.

'Bloody Mary,' Joel said, lifting his head. Norbert's ears pricked up. 'Extra Tabasco. Extra vodka too, if they'll do it.' He groaned and stretched his head backwards. 'That extra tequila was a mistake last night.'

'How about you, Norbert?'

Norbert, who was still staring at Joel's arched neck, didn't answer at first.

'Hey, Norbert! What's your poison?'

'Hemlock, normally,' Norbert said. It was one of the things he'd wanted to buy in the shop, he suddenly remembered.

Laughter rippled around the table.

'Nice one' said Cameron. 'Really though, what do you

want to drink?'

A sudden flash of colour caught Norbert's attention, and he turned towards the bar, his eyes fixed on it like radar. As he watched the barman pour a thick, red liquid from a jug into a glass he could feel his fangs starting to tremble.

He pointed towards the bar, and tried to keep his voice light. 'Could I trouble you for one of those?' he asked.

'Heavy night for you too was it, Norbert mate?' asked Joel, who had followed Norbert's gaze. He turned to Cameron.

'If there's two of us, you may as well get a jug.'

By the time Cameron returned with the drinks, Norbert was sweating in anticipation. Forgetting all rules of etiquette, he grabbed the first glass Cameron poured and slurped greedily.

The first mouthful was a crushing disappointment, and Norbert slumped back in his chair. He should have known better than to expect the real thing, he realised, as he surveyed the room. Anyone could see that this wasn't his sort of place. The crowd of people who were scattered in small groups around the bar, chatting and laughing with each other, would have been horrified to know what he had been hoping to find in that glass. His companions, too. He shouldn't be here.

Glumly, he took another sip of his drink. It was actually quite pleasant, he realised; although it lacked the metallic tang he'd been hoping for, there was a nice peppery flavour, and it had quite a kick at the end. The next mouthful left him with a light buzzy feeling between his ears. Norbert felt himself beginning to relax, and took another sip.

By his third glass, Norbert had cheered up considerably. He had taken off his tie, his waistcoat was slightly askew and he was listening to Cameron and Joel having a heated debate about whether or not swans had teeth. The young people really were quite good company. Annabelle had been acting a bit coolly towards him, but then she didn't seem to say much to any of the others either. Except for Joel, who she kept looking at when she thought no-one was watching. But Cameron and Joel and the girl with the neck – Suzie was her name, he remembered – had been perfectly pleasant. Perhaps the day wasn't such a disaster after all.

'I'm telling you for the last time, they do.' Joel was beginning to slur his words. 'Pointy buggers. My mate reckons he got bitten by one once. Anyway –' he drained the last of his drink and pointed at the empty jug, where ice cubes were melting into a pale, plasma-like puddle. 'Shall we have another?'

'Please, allow me' Norbert said, producing a wad of cash from his pocket. After all, it's not as if I've got anywhere to spend this now.' Joel took the money, and rose to his feet. 'Thanks mate. Let me go, though. I've got my eye on that barmaid.' He winked and walked a little unsteadily to the bar.

Annabelle immediately stood up as well. 'I think I'll go out for a smoke,' she said, with a frown. 'Anyone coming?'

Cameron went with her, and Norbert found himself alone with Suzie.

'Can I ask you a question?' she said. As she turned towards him, he couldn't resist another look at her neck. She had taken her coat off when they entered the pub, and was wearing a tiny silver crucifix on a chain. Seeing it twinkle from between her collar bones Norbert felt almost relieved. The last thing he needed now was for his impulses to get the better of him. Suzie's necklace meant one less temptation.

'By all means.'

'Why doesn't your skin sparkle?'

'My skin?'

'It's just that – well, there's this book I'm reading,' she looked embarrassed. 'The vampire in it has this really sparkly skin, like glitter. I just sort of assumed you'd all have it.'

A shiver crept up Norbert's spine; there was no mistaking the word she had used. He looked down at the table.

'I'm aware there are stories,' he said, in a quiet voice.

'Although I don't think I'm familiar with the particular one you have been reading. Most of them contain a certain amount of –' he searched for the right word, 'misinformation.'

'But some of it must be true. That fruit and vegetable stall we passed on the way here – it was the garlic, wasn't it? The reason you crossed the street?'

'Yes' said Norbert. 'Garlic does cause some issues. As do those.' He pointed at Suzie's necklace.

'God, sorry – I'd completely forgotten I was wearing this,' said Suzie, her fingers reaching for the necklace. 'I can take it off, if you like.' She lifted her hands to her neck and started to undo the clasp.

'It's probably best if you leave it on,' Norbert said, rather more quickly than he meant to.

Suzie's hands froze for a moment, then dropped back into her lap. 'So that part's true,' she said quietly. 'You do drink –'

'Yes. I'm afraid so.' Norbert could feel her eyes on him, but couldn't bring himself to meet them.

'What about the others. Do they need protection too?'

Norbert looked over at Joel, who was talking to the girl behind the bar. She had bright pink hair and a ring through her nose.

'It really would be most impolite to attack any of you, after you've provided such splendid company.' Norbert said. He pulled out the silver hip flask he kept in his top pocket. 'I keep an emergency supply for – situations like this.'

'I see,' said Susie, glancing nervously at the flask. A barman came to clear away their empty glasses and frowned at Norbert, who stuffed the flask back into his pocket.

'Perhaps I should go,' he said, after a long silence.

'Please don't. Joel's just ordered another round of drinks, and –' Suzie paused. 'Really. It's okay if you want to stay.'

Norbert nodded. 'Very well,' he said. 'But if I am to stay, it might be best not to mention –' he gestured towards

Annabelle and Cameron, who were smoking on the other side of a nearby window.

'Not a word,' said Suzie. 'As long as you don't let on that I've been reading those books. I'd never hear the end of it.'

Norbert considered this. 'It's a deal,' he said and then chuckled to himself. 'I thought I'd heard everything, but 'sparkly skin' is a new one. Those ridiculous stories people keep writing will be the death of me one day.'

Suzie smiled.

'Aren't you already dead?' she asked.

Norbert thought for a moment. 'Technically, yes. I suppose I am'.

He wasn't sure why this was so funny, but for some reason it was, and a surge of laughter bubbled up uncontrollably inside him. Suzie seemed to find it hilarious too and before long they were both in fits of hysterics. It was an unfamiliar sensation; Norbert's sides ached and he gasped great breaths of air as he tried to control himself. Every time he managed to regain some composure he would catch Suzie's eye which set them both off again.

'What's so funny?' Joel arrived back from the bar with a jug in one hand and a tray of glasses in the other.

'Nothing,' spluttered Suzie, winking at Norbert. 'Just watching you crash and burn with that barmaid.' Joel quickly began to pour the drinks. 'She's not really my type anyway,' he mumbled.

'Might I be so bold as to suggest you shift your romantic intentions a little, er, closer to home?' Norbert said, and nodded towards the window.

Joel raised his eyebrows, then shook his head.

'Annabelle? She's way out of my league.'

'Perhaps. Although she looked a little aggrieved when you mentioned your interest in the other,' he looked over at the bar, where the pink-haired girl was showing one of the customers a tattoo on her arm, 'young lady'.

'Really?' Joel brightened a little and his gaze returned to

the window as he passed Norbert a fresh glass. 'Cheers, man.' They clinked their glasses together. Barely a minute had passed before Joel set his down again.

'I could do with a quick fag too, now I think about it,' he muttered, and headed outside.

Norbert spent the rest of the afternoon leaning back in his chair, with a contented, slightly lopsided smile on his face. As one hour blurred into the next his head began to feel slightly fuzzy, and he forgot all about his attempted shopping trip. In his top pocket, the flask remained untouched. Eventually, he became dimly aware that the conversation around him had turned to food.

'I could murder a bowl of pho,' Annabelle announced.

Joel nodded in enthusiastic agreement.

'Me too,' he said. 'Everyone happy with Vietnamese?'

Norbert searched for his pocket-watch.

'What time is it?' he asked, after dropping it for the second time.

Suzie consulted her phone.

'Half past four,' she replied, and Norbert rubbed his eyes.

'Gracious,' he said. 'I suppose I really ought to be getting back'.

'We'll be walking back towards the station anyway,' Suzie said, as they spilled out onto the pavement. 'You may change your mind when we get to the restaurant.'

Annabelle took the lead, and Joel quickened his pace to join her, deftly managing to separate them both slightly from the rest of the group. Norbert smiled. He was sure he was right about those two.

'You know, Norbert, for someone who doesn't even have a heart, you're quite the romantic,' said Suzie, taking his arm as she followed his gaze.

Norbert smiled at her. 'The missing hearts are another myth, I'm afraid. I'm pleased to say that mine is entirely present and accounted for. Although, perhaps not quite as accounted for as I'd like it to be.' He hadn't really meant to say that last part out loud.

'You don't have a girlfriend? Or a wife?'

Norbert shook his head.

'But there must have been someone, once. What happened?'

Norbert thought about the empty shop. One visit every thirty years really wasn't very much, now that he thought about it.

'I didn't make enough effort, I suppose.'

'And it's too late for some kind of reconciliation?'

'I'm not sure I'd even know where to find her now.'

Suzie squeezed him arm gently.

'Maybe she'll turn up again someday,' she said.

'Perhaps,' replied Norbert.

They stopped a few moments later in front of a green shop front. Its windows were plastered in stickers and copies of magazine reviews. 'We're here,' said Suzie. '*Beit Hu*. Hands down, the best pho in Hoxton. Are you sure you won't stay for some food?'

'That's very kind,' said Norbert, 'but I really do think I should be off.' He turned to the others.

'I'm sorry not to dining with you,' he said.

Annabelle waved a vague goodbye then disappeared into the restaurant and Cameron shook Norbert by the hand. 'Nice to meet you, fella.'

'Yeah,' added Joel. 'It's been cool.'

'Quite,' said Norbert, returning Joel's smile. 'Good luck, by the way.' He tipped his head towards the restaurant door. Joel blushed. 'I might just see if she's found a table,' he muttered.

Norbert turned to Suzie. 'Thank you for a delightful afternoon,' he said, and kissed her hand. 'It has been a great pleasure to make your acquaintance.'

'For me as well,' said Suzie. 'I'm sorry you can't stay.'

'So am I,' said Norbert. 'But thank you. For everything.'

'My pleasure,' said Suzie. She paused for a moment, then pecked him on the cheek, and disappeared inside the restaurant.

Norbert watched through the window as she joined the others, then turned towards the station. *Biet Hu*. He'd have to remember that.

Perhaps he'd come back again in November after all, Norbert thought to himself as he boarded the train. Maybe he could take Lucinda out for a drink after she finished work. He'd explain to her about the Bloody Marys before she tried one, so that she wouldn't be disappointed, and maybe afterwards they could try a bowl of this 'pho' the young people had been talking about. He wasn't entirely sure what it was, he realised, as he closed his eyes and the train rocked its steady, soothing rhythm. But just for once, it couldn't hurt to try something new.

SHOREDITCH HIGH STREET

The Horror, the Horror
Katy Darby

Bombastic, off Brick Lane, is Mumbai slum chic with a Bollywood twist: cocktails are named after tropical diseases of the gut, and 6-7 p.m. is Hopi Hour, because the owner got confused about the Indian theme. But it's near Charlie's office, and Sedge works here part-time, so that's where the meeting happens.

April, twenty-seven, wears thrift-shop vintage from Chicago, Balinese funeral jewellery, and children's trainers by George at ASDA. Her heavy-framed specs are plain glass since she had her eyes lasered last year: she's aware of the irony. April is (what else?) an independent film director. I know what you're thinking, but gentle reader, forbear; you cannot possibly hate April more than she'll come to hate herself, and that's a promise.

Charlie's twenty-eight, but thanks to his edgy, vibrant lifestyle (coke washed down with triple-Sagatibas, Marlboro Mediums and Red Bull for breakfast) looks ten years older. He wears sunglasses all the time; partly for the look but mostly to hide his pink ping-pong eyeballs. He's rake-thin and lamp-post tall; a beacon of blagging debauchery. Charlie is a producer-slash-editor. He's made mostly ads and virals so far; for websites, boutiques, pop-up magazines, festivals, and girls he's trying to sleep with. He wants to get into bed with April – sweet, petite, minor-award-winning April – in more ways than one, so he's agreed to work on The Project.

Sedge is not his real name. He grew up in Preston,

Lancashire, a place no other screenwriters, to his knowledge, ever hailed from, and up there parents call their children by sensible, commonplace names from the Bible, or else generations-old family names: which is why his full name is Bernard Sedgewick and also, not uncoincidentally, why he insists on being called Sedge. He's written two unproduced screenplays, four webisodes of *Skins,* and a short about mortician-beauticians called *Anal Glue*, the rough cut of which vanished, a victim of Arts Council belt-tightening, before post-production, its existence as brief and beautiful as a butterfly's dream.

The Project came to Sedge in a blinding flash one Cointreau-fuelled night in Shoreditch House and he immediately took it to April, who'd assistant-directed *Anal Glue*, because he knew she was looking for the Next Big Thing and he was anxiously certain, somehow, that this was it. Sedge, with typical writer's inarticulacy, only pitched it to her after six Japanese beers and half a joint smoked furtively on the East Rooms terrace, but she instantly grasped its importance and promised, serious-browed, to *give it her all* and really *punch it home*. Sedge gets shudders at the thought of doll-like April doing either of these things, and he's sunk a thousand pounds of his compensation money (don't ask) to get her on board.

After several rounds of Yellow Fevers and a pitcher of Dengue, Charlie, Sedge and April are very excited about The Project indeed.

I'm very excited, says Charlie, dully. After years of negotiating deals with only balls and bullshit on his side, the more boring Charlie's voice gets, the more interested he is. April's never heard him so monotone: she knows this means that this is *it,* the big one, the showcase, the break. The one that gets you places: Sundance, Cannes, even (whisper it!) BAFTA. So she's excited too, and lays it on the line.

The thing is, April says urgently, this is like major shit. Am I right, Charlie?

Charlie, returning from the toilet for the sixth time, nods, twitches, and sniffs. Sedge hopes their producer's not developing a cold.

Right, says April. And Sedge is a major talent, no doubt.

Major, agrees Charlie.

I promise you, Sedge, says April, we'll take your wonderful, beautiful script and turn it into –

A shitload of money! yelps Charlie, his ennui suddenly burned away, along with half his septum.

April silences him with a glare through Kerouac frames. Something we can all be *proud* of. Yeah?

Sedge nods. Charlie's head bobs, though whether in agreement or in time to the bhangra 'n' bass, it's hard to tell.

So, she says. The first thing we need to do, once we've done casting and locations and shit, is to purge all the crap ideas and impulses and bad art that creep into this whole, fucking, *life* of ours, yeah? Her slender, bangled arm indicates the whole of Shoreditch. The Project has to be *pure*, OK? Untainted by commercialism, hackneyed ideas, clichés and banality. This baby has to sing. It has to be all it can be, yeah? You up for that?

She leans eagerly over the low table, and her small, mesmerising gymnast's breasts nose forwards like inquisitive rabbits under her cut-off Thomas Pink shirt. Sedge and Charlie nod. They are *definitely* up for that.

*

It's Day One of brainstorming. They're in a Stepney warehouse Charlie woke up in once after a midsummer rave; it seems to be abandoned so they've made it their office-cum-studio and will be filming the dream sequences here. It's fucking freezing, but Charlie's Coffee Surprise (the surprise is the gin) warms Sedge's entrails in what may not turn out to be a good way.

Two flipcharts, says April, standing in front of them like General Franco's middle-management facilitator, a marker in either hand. On my left: good ideas. Sensitive, real, truthful, pure. On my right: shit ones. Crass, commercial, Michael Bay, Richard Curtis mass-feeding pap. We all have them; let's not be afraid. Shout them out, yeah?

There's an embarrassed silence. Charlie looks confused, and Sedge, whose septic tank of shit ideas normally overflows, is dumbstruck.

War and horror, right? says April. But not as we know it. We're making *psychological* horror, naturally, holding the cracked mirror up to the inhumanity that is man – wait a sec, that's quite good … She scribbles it on the virgin sheet to her left. Where was I? Oh yeah, *true* horror. We're going to shock and scare the viewer, in a good way obviously, but what the *public* associates with war and horror films is *Friday the 13th*, Freddy Kruger-style dross. Yeah? So we're going to clean our heads out of all this bullshit, starting with *you*.

She fires her marker at Charlie.

I liked *Alien*, he says, hesitantly.

Yes, April says impatiently, we all liked *Alien*. *Alien* is good. What's bad? I'm looking for *bad* here, Chuckie.

Alien3, says Sedge suddenly. His brain creaks into gear. With the clones. Charles Dance bangs Sigourney Weaver. That bloke off *Who's The Boss*, he's in it.

April winces. Joe McGann? That's the stuff. She writes CLONES and MCGANN (ANY) on the right-hand flipchart.

Nazis! says Charlie suddenly, grinning as if in fond recollection.

Jaws 2! Sedge adds. Any film with sharks! April scrawls industriously. Sedge is warming up, starting to enjoy this game. Their mental sewers have miraculously unblocked, and he and Charlie let the shit gush.

Trenches! cries Charlie. The girlfriend's photo in his pocket. The gruff sergeant with a heart of gold. The um, goose-stepping, leather trench coat, Gestapo guys with duelling scars.

Even Sedge clocks that Charlie has segued straight from

First to Second World War, apparently without realising, but April doesn't seem to care. After three hours, and two more refills of Coffee Surprise, they have eight flipchart pages of rubbish ideas and one (widely-spaced) of good ones.

See? says April. How *easy* it is to come up with crap? How tough it is to keep the good stuff *pure*?

Charlie and Sedge nod like schoolboys astonished into learning something.

The sheet on the left says:

Gay conscientious objector stretcher-bearer in WWI.

Addicted to the morphine he uses on the dying.

Pain of life too much to bear (metaphor too obvious?)

Dies during Christmas Day football match, saving Germans' equalising goal.

The right-hand one sports a chaos of hoary shocker ideas, including Nazis, sharks, aliens, serial-killers, anything to do with the Vatican or ancient texts, cyborgs, time-travel, genetic engineering and clowns.

That side, April explains, is the shittiest pile of money-spinning, lowest-common-denominator *trash* Hollywood ever optioned. We'll call it – she glances briefly, contemptuously, over the list of tropes: *Nazi Sharks in a Trench*. And into that trench is where we'll throw every commercial, sell-out, humdrum idea we have.

And on the left, says April softly, is the film we know we can make. The film we *must* make. The *vision* we all share. And the name of that film is (she looks at Sedge, inclining her head like a worshipful geisha) *Unbearable*.

*

As filming begins, Sedge has never been so thrilled. April has never been so creatively fulfilled. And Charlie has never done so much coke. He gets everyone he knows in a froth of near-sexual excitement about *Unbearable*: about the tears it'll jerk, the awards it'll win, the proles it will enlighten and ultimately (for isn't that, after all, the real point?) the names it will make, to wit: his.

Every shit idea they have, they dutifully channel into Nazi Sharks, their imaginary big-budget dick-flick. The crew joins in enthusiastically (Robot sharks! Genetically-modified Nazis! Kung-Fu aliens!) and the right-hand flipchart gets fuller. Slowly, surely, *Unbearable,* that poem of a film, that elegant, Mozartian symphony of celluloid, freighted with anomie, filigreed with heart-clenching melancholy, is made – or makes itself, *dreams* itself into being with light and shadow, as April sometimes thinks at 4 a.m. on a night shoot, fired by Charlie's inspiration powder. Sedge is awed by her; by the process, by the fact that an idea inspired by his great-granddad's war stories over Boxing Day turkey is opening like a flower; and it's more beautiful than he could ever have imagined.

The night before the premiere, at a semi-derelict indie bingo hall, Charlie invites Sedge and April and the crew round to his to watch the final cut. Into the hushed silence afterwards, he throws a single glittering DVD, another couple of grainy white Baggies, and a gleaming, cranked-up smile.

I couldn't sleep last night, he says, and I've got a surprise for everyone.

He and Sedge (on a mash-up of ketamine, speed and Ginster's pasties) have cut together the out-takes and deleted scenes of *Unbearable* with some out-of-copyright footage from the Discovery and History channels, and this is the result: a two-minute trailer for *Nazi Sharks in a Trench*.

*

Have you guessed it? Perhaps, the world being what it is, you have. For while *Unbearable* and director April are duly BAFTA-nominated, it's the trailer for *Nazi Sharks* that goes viral, finding its way to the tablet of one exceptionally successful director of blockbusters, who options it, brokering an unprecedented writer-producer deal with its 'fearsomely talented' (*Newsweek*) co-creators Charlie Morris and Bernard Sedgewick.

It's Charlie and Sedge who benefit from the tie-in sales, the action figures, the Happy Meal giveaways, the t-shirts, the willing groupies, and the fawning interviews on highly-rated chat shows. But who, in the end, is the richer? The girl who stuck to her guns, directing low-budget art films for little pay and less recognition, or the boys who made it big at the expense of a shell-sized hole in their souls?

Perhaps neither, perhaps both, thinks April, as she glances across the studio to where Jonathan Ross sits, sporting an official t-shirt on which Morgan Freeman as General Haig scowls over the stencilled legend: GET THOSE MOTHERFUCKING SHARKS OUTTA MY MOTHERFUCKING TRENCH! She's here to talk about her forthcoming no-holds-barred tell-all, *Nazi Sharks: The Uncut Story*. What did you expect? This is the movies: everybody sells out in the end.

Besides, she's planning to use the book money to fund her latest project, the one that'll win her long-coveted BAFTA: perhaps even a Palm d'Or or a Golden Bear? It's a story based on something Sedge told her one night shoot about his other grandfather, a deaf-mute Jewish cabinetmaker who escaped from Stalin's Russia by pretending to be a French mime.

And this time she's not leaving anything to chance. She's going to write, direct and produce it solo: her vision will remain unsullied by sharks, Nazi or otherwise. *Unspeakable* will be hers alone: pure, and beautiful. And Oscar fucking *gold*.

WHITECHAPEL

Lenny Bolton Changes Trains
Rob Walton

Lenny Bolton found himself face-down in the entrance to Whitechapel Station with a tomato, brie and avocado baguette raised, almost triumphantly, in the air.

He stood up, looked around, and rubbed his left hand around his stubble. With his right hand Lenny wedged his sandwich in his pocket, then asked a young man in a green hoodie with some indecipherable script on the front what was going on.

'Flash mob. Whitechapel Gallery.'

Lenny was, as his dad would have said, none the wiser.

He turned to ask a woman – another hoodie, no writing – and her response made a bit more sense.

'Come and join us, we're a flash mob meeting here before we process down to Whitechapel Art Gallery to do an unveiling outside.'

Christ, there were a few verbal oddities to come to terms with there. Process? Must be as in procession. Flash mobs? Perhaps he hadn't wanted to acknowledge the phrase when the man answered, but now realised he had read about them; he'd seen a video of some people spontaneously bursting into song in a café somewhere. But what was the unveiling she was talking about? They probably had something stuck up their hoodies. Maybe something would happen so all that weird writing would make sense. Maybe it was an alternative alphabet. The fact was it could be just about anything.

Lenny had lots of friends who thought art was basically oil paintings and the annual weirdness of the Turner Prize. He'd been to the Turner Prize exhibition one year and was surprised by how much he understood. He got it.

He pulled the sandwich from his pocket, noting the avocado which preferred to stay in his jacket, went to take a bite and realised that the girl in the hoodie was still looking at him: she looked as though she had been waiting.

'Well? Are you coming?'

'I, er, I can't. I work here. Not always, just now. I'm doing a job here. I'm on my lunch break.'

'What's your job?'

'Er, paving. I'm putting down the tactile paving for the visually impaired. Not always. Just today. Sometimes I put down the other stuff, but today it just happens to be the tactile stuff, you know – the flags with the raised bobbles and that, so people with, er, vision issues, can feel, with their feet, how close they are to the tracks, to the end, to the edge of the platform.'

And from that messy conversation Leonard Stephen Bolton, thirty-two years old and single, found himself part of a flash mob, leaving the station where he had been working for the past week. He was, as he had told the young woman (what was her name?) on his lunch break anyway, but he found himself looking behind, wondering if his colleagues (hang on, weren't they his workmates?) were watching. He paused outside the station, under the fancy modern canopy which he found a bit strange and incongruous against the old building.

'Why there?'

'Pardon?'

'Why Whitechapel Gallery? And what's your name? I'm Lenny. Lenny Bolton.'

They seemed to have stopped outside the station while the people in the front had a cigarette. This didn't seem much of a flash mob to Lenny, he thought they were all about speed, stealth, surprise. (His words and thoughts were emerging in some weird bastardised triplicate.)

'We want to show the other side of Whitechapel. There have been TV programmes about the area, the things that have gone on here. There are always books about Jack the Ripper, about that side of things. We want people to associate Whitechapel with art above all.'

'But there isn't just one other side of the area, is there? There are any number of sides.' His speech was becoming more natural now, he wasn't so awed. He could stand up and be counted. 'I actually live down the road. I know there are many sides to this area. I even know many sides to this station. What about you? Where do you live? And what's your name?'

'I live...a bit further.' A shared smile. 'This is just a start.'

'Oh?'

'Come on.'

She headed back in to the station, seeming not to care about the flash mob who were finishing their cigarettes and looking determined again. She seemed to instinctively go down the stairs to the platform where he'd been laying the flags. She explained that there was a plan to put paintings and sculptures all over the station in another flash mob the following week, once the fuss had died down. Lenny explained to her the folly of placing sculptures down there at the same time as he was laying flagstones to help the visually impaired get around with more ease.

'You can't just dump sculptures in a public place. Whoever is in charge of these flash mobs hasn't thought it through. Think about what I'm doing. And another thing. Shouldn't it be up to the people of Whitechapel what impression they give of the area. Not – not outsiders.'

'What's the most beautiful thing you've ever seen?'

'What?'

'What's the most beautiful thing you've ever seen?'

'Probably – '

'Or tasted or smelt or heard or felt?'

'I – '

'Sorry. I want to get to know you – or something of you – quickly.'

'Having a list of my likes isn't really getting to know me, is it? It's the sort of thing where you get rehearsed answers in magazine questionnaires. It can all be a bit superficial.'

He paused, before looking into her eyes and saying,

'I'm Lenny, Lenny Bolton. And your name is…?'

She laughed.

'Those slabs, are they – ?'

'They're called tactile. I think I told you. You know – '

'To do with touch.'

'That's right.'

'If you don't have one sense the others are more highly developed.'

'Is that actually true? I know people say it, but is it, you know, a fact?'

'Well…'

'Think about the different senses.'

The conversation carried on for another five minutes, leaving his head full, whirring. He gave her his phone number and she gave him hers, but she only laughed again when he asked for her name. He wasn't sure what to type in so he wrote Whitechapel Art Gal, as though it was an abbreviation. It amused him.

Lenny made his tea that night as he listened to Radio 4. He ate it as he walked round his flat, thinking; dreaming; scheming. He decided he wanted to do something at the station, some artwork. He looked at the prints on his walls, the books on his shelves. He walked, eating his pasta as he looked at CDs and DVDs for inspiration. He had very few ornaments, but those he did have he examined in case inspiration could be found by staring at something and hoping.

He had no idea how *Where's Wally* came into his head. It was completely unbidden. He drank a bottle of Grolsch as he looked out of his window, thinking how *Where's Lenny* was going to work as a piece of art when his phone vibrated. A text from Whitechapel Art Gal: 'Which artist said 'We are here to show the world to the unworldly'?'

'Come again?' he said to the flat, to the phone, to the world outside the window.

Another text from the same source: 'More soon. X'

An 'X'. Was there one of those on the last text?

Five minutes later another one. 'Painting is the most noble of all the visual arts. Photography is both the most public and the most private.'

He didn't have a clue what that was supposed to mean. He texted back, 'I had simple pasta with basil, olive oil and parmesan. What's your name?'

No other texts came in, so he turned his phone off and went for a bath with a notebook – which could double as a sketch book if the mood took him. The *Where's Lenny* idea had fallen apart before it had been fully formed. Some vague notion of putting photos of himself in print-outs of Old Masters and sticking them to the pillars in the station was abandoned.

He thought of many ideas for paintings which he could stick to the pillars, thought of sticking things on the treads of the staircases. He knew they wouldn't last but maybe there was something about the impermanence. Something to do with Whitechapel Station changing, being a place of change, a place where people passed through.

He thought of going down later that night. Could he go in his work gear, carrying rolls of pictures to be pasted up on pillars? He could stick paintings to all the columns, write ART in spray paint, emulsion, gloss, with a small paintbrush. In lots of different ways. He could try to do some Braille (he had no idea how to start). He could write on the tactile paving slabs. He finished his beer and dismissed it as silly, fanciful. He was getting tired; too much had happened in one day, too much had happened in one head.

The flash mobs communicated by texts and tweets, which was great in lots of ways, but something different was needed for a train station. There was too much hurrying, too many things done at speed without proper human contact. He needed to do something to slow things down, to get people to stay in the station and think. He wanted people to go to the station to do something other than boarding a train.

He got out of the bath and got in bed without bothering with clothes. He fell asleep with two new ideas crashing round his head. He slept off and on for six hours, red spots and grey suits flickering through his dreams.

*

The theory goes that if you give a group of monkeys some paint, paintbrushes and canvases it would take an absolute age to clean up the mess. It would be a disaster. This morning Lenny Bolton looked in the mirror and felt he looked like something that had been painted by those monkeys. He was a bit messy.

The ideas he'd had as he fell asleep had changed. He'd been thinking of mounting artworks such as paintings inside the station. Then he thought he could go along the paintings, posters and sculptures, carefully placing little red dots on about a third, Not For Sale (NFS) stickers on a third and leaving a third blank. If he managed to get away with any of that he could do the next stage at lunchtime.

But why couldn't people look at what was already there? He could feel his ideas taking form and shape, perhaps like those of an artist take shape and form.

He went in to the station the following morning with more ideas than he'd had in years.

He did his work for about an hour, getting into a rhythm and smiling, thinking ahead, thinking wide, far and deep. He considered the possibility of wrapping up Whitechapel Station – the Overground and the Underground linked together. He'd need to leave it a while; let the dust settle on this one. How did you cover such big buildings, big structures? How did you get such big sheets of anything? Or did you use lots of smaller bits? He was taking his inspiration from that bloke who wrapped up buildings. Was his name Christophe? Something like that.

He interrupted himself. Of course! He was coming at this from entirely the wrong angle. He texted Whitechapel Art Gal: 'Clarity has arrived. I was making a Rodin for my own Braque.'

The art shouldn't be all this paraphernalia, all these solid things for sale. He was the art, the station was the art. The station was the gallery. He was curator, caretaker and guide.

In his lunch break he ran to W H Smith, where he picked up some red dot stickers and some plain white ones.

He'd seen those men and women in various galleries over the years. When he'd been on school trips, or seen them in old films, they always used to wear a formal uniform: suit and peaked cap. Now it would often be dark trousers and a polo shirt adorned with the gallery logo, possibly even a slogan. He decided he'd have to go down the more formal route, otherwise he'd just look like a bloke waiting for a train to take him to a gallery – or a gallery groupie, if such people existed.

He had a grey suit at home.

He texted her, asking if she could come to the station to do him a favour. She turned up ten minutes later. He gave her the key to his flat and some money. This was not how he usually behaved, but things were changing. Things were changing very quickly.

She returned mid-afternoon with a bulging and bulky carrier bag. He took it into the toilet staff and visiting workers were allowed to use. When he came out she had placed either a 'Sold' red dot or 'NFS' sticker on each pillar, banister and bench. She had placed them on every structure and piece of furniture available. He took the folded shooting stick from the bag, and sat on it against a pillar, looking at the commuters, visitors, day-trippers. He sat looking at the visitors to his gallery, contemplating going up to them to ask what they thought of the tactile paving flags, the bins, the direction signs.

She stood a short distance away, smiling.

After ten minutes, when people started to work out something was afoot, he went up to her and described their relationship and how it might pan out. There would be an early period characterised by installations and performances, then a conventional middle period. If she was interested this would be followed by a strange naïve period and, well, after that it was up to her.

'What did you say your name was?'

SHADWELL

Rich and Strange
Bartle Sawbridge

There were only three punters left now, a couple and a lone woman – probably divorced with a good settlement – and they were all listening to the intruders, locals, residents, whatever you wanted to call them, instead of listening to him. Phil pulled up the zip of his high viz jacket a little further as the April mist settled on his hair and face. The water in Shadwell Basin was muddy grey. He could have made more sales sitting in his office than were likely to come from this mess.

*

He had been so excited. It was a first, taking a group of punters out together to see the range of properties on offer in Shadwell. His idea, too, definite brownie points in the office – you could tell from the snide remarks about 'wasting a good Saturday evening'. He had written a script and memorised it. And it had started so well. Arrived in plenty of time and the early evening sun had gained lustre as it flashed through the metal and glass of the City, and planted orange 'Sold' signs on every apartment window that it met. After the nervous minutes of 'no-one's going to turn up', two or three became ten, then twelve, and at the peak Phil counted eighteen: couples, straight and single-sex, with a few singles, mostly older, downsizing from the empty nest probably.

Phil and his group were watched as they stood between the stations and Watney Street market, by people sitting on their usual bench, or out for a stroll before dark, or picking up some late shopping, and veg being given away as the last stalls closed in the market. With his Rich & Strange Estate Agent's logo on his big yellow jacket obscured by the group, it was hard to tell what he and they were – a sergeant training up some new police support officers? Unlikely; some of the group looked stiff in their fitted casual clothes, and most of them wore the scent of money, recognisable even at this distance.

Phil introduced himself and started to address his group about the range and quality of houses and apartments in this area just east of the City.

'Of course, all of this area was badly hit by the Blitz, which accounts for the variety of architectural styles – some maybe more attractive than others – but then, that's reflected in the price of course, so there are bargains to be had if you look for them.'

Two stallholders in the market starting shouting across the street to each other, so that Phil had to stop speaking. The group of home seekers stared at them with annoyance: *who were these people,* their faces said, *to interrupt an evening sacrificed to self-betterment?*

'Anyway,' continued Phil, with a little laugh, 'it's really quite peaceful round here, I'm happy to say. Low crime rate, little violence, but most important, easy access to the City, Canary Wharf, the West End, Stratford with all its potential, and even south-east London – all thanks to the DLR and the Overground. Where could be better to put down roots?' This question was drowned out by a plane going low overhead to land at City Airport. 'Right on cue,' beamed Phil, 'just down the road for flights to Europe's business centres.'

A small man, with a round face and round glasses, not one of the watchers, walked quickly from the DLR station straight towards the group.

Phil, spotting a potential recruit, called 'Why not join us, we're looking at Shadwell as it was, as it is now, and – especially – as it will be very soon with the help of Rich & Strange.'

'I thought there would at least be a plaque. There isn't one at either of the stations,' was the small man's response. Mistaking the resulting silence for interest, or maybe not even noticing it, he went on: 'most of them are stacked up so tight in Westminster Abbey that some of them are standing, gets boring it's so easy, but Shadwell? Nothing. Okay, I know he didn't come from here, but they must have named the place after him.'

'Sorry,' said Phil, 'I thought you were joining my tour of property purchasing opportunities in the area.'

'Oh, no, Poets Laureate. Part of my London A to Z. Have to find a visible London connection for each Poet Laureate. Got to Dryden, that was easy, but bloody Shadwell, pardon my French.'

'Why don't you just move on to the next poet?'

'Can't. Not allowed. May have to abandon it. Move on to Q. O was Observatories, N was Necromancy – Q is Queens. More Westminster Abbey, of course, but there should be some variety, and documentation. The Tower! A few ended up there.' No-one asked him about A to M.

'Right, better be off. DLR straight to Tower Gateway. Let Q commence!' and he was gone.

'Well, good luck to him,' laughed Phil, 'and now back to business. It's a diverse area round here.'

'Well, yes and no,' said one of the lookers-on, an Asian man in warm trousers, a thick jumper and a knitted beanie who had approached the group.

'Please, sir,' said Phil, 'can't you see – ?'

'No,' said a young woman near the front of the group, 'I'm interested to hear what he says.'

'Thank you, madam. I am Ahmed, by the way. You see, the community round here predominantly has its roots in Bangladesh. If you pass the primary school over there during playtime you won't see a white face. But the City people who come and buy properties here,' looking pleasantly at Phil's group, 'they don't spend any time here, and they don't spend any money here. They just sleep here. They could bring diversity, but they don't want to. They only want to be here so that they can get somewhere else quickly.'

But the group didn't see community; they saw ex-council two-beds at two hundred thousand pounds, a snip if you were prepared to put up with the drab surroundings. Proper communities came expensive, like the one Phil had taken them to off Cable Street, where the outer gates guarded the inner ones, which protected the residents inside, and their aspirations, from contagion; aspirations to move back to Hampshire or Buckinghamshire when bigger bonuses and children arrived. Or maybe it was a short prison term before they were released to their inheritance.

'Look Phil,' said a tall, dark-haired man standing at the back of the group, 'can't you do anything about these interruptions? We've come here to look at properties, not take abuse from local troublemakers.'

'Yes,' agreed a woman in a denim suit in front of him,

'I had to refuse a dinner party to come here.'

'There's not a lot more to show you just here…' said Phil.

'This isn't even Shadwell,' said a new voice. A strange looking woman had joined the group, who looked at Phil for help. 'Shadwell's down by the Basin and the river.'

'Not another one,' cried the dark-haired man, 'that does it for me,' and he took his partner by the hand and walked away.

'That's just where we're going,' said Phil, embarrassed by the defection, and by this woman no doubt appearing to the group as if she had taken over the tour. 'Follow me', he said, trying to restore his authority.

They followed him past the stations, east along Cable Street and then south, to where there were more ex-council blocks.

'Look,' said Phil, 'they're adding on to the estates.' He waved an arm at where development work was turning old green spaces into more apartments. 'Rich & Strange hasn't got this one, but you can see what the demand's like.'

The new woman was walking alongside the group. Most of them turned inwards, ignoring her and the side road running through Shadwell as fast as it could, and spoke to each other:

'It's not just a place to sleep; it's got to work for me, otherwise I can rent and get into equities,'

'He's not said much about yields. I might buy a couple and rent one out if the margins are right.'

'The transport links are great – I could run to work in ten minutes. But he hasn't convinced me this isn't a dodgy area.'

But a few of them were more curious, and glanced at the woman more closely as she kept pace with them. She was wearing tight pale blue jeans, and an orange and pink kameez with a low neckline and slits up either side. Her head was uncovered, but the overall impression was still of traditional Muslim dress.

As they approached Shadwell Basin she said: 'My great-great or whatever granddad wound up here in eighteen sixty something from India and couldn't get a ship back. Happened to thousands of them, the sailors were hired for a single journey, and had to hope they could pick up another ship going back.'

'Now, look at this', exclaimed Phil, trying once more to regain control, and including the houses round two sides of the Basin with a sweep of his arm, 'something to make the mouth water if the pocket's deep enough. Don't come on the market often though.'

'Those Mickey Mouse fake warehouses he's pointing at,' said the woman, 'that's where the sailors used to put up – tenements and hostels, a dozen to a room. Most of them died. My old chap must have got lucky. He married a Scottish woman, 'that's why they call me Maggie,' she hammered in Cockney Glaswegian.

' ...and there's water sports for all tastes, canoeing, kayaking...' said Phil desperately.

'...and dinghy captains in peaked Barbour caps.' Maggie countered.

A few of the group laughed, and the rest protested. Someone said, 'Who's coming to the pub?' and five people followed him. Others turned back towards the stations, leaving only the couple and the woman on her own listening to Maggie.

*

'There's the river,' Maggie said, 'where everyone came from. It sucks people in and drops them on land until they can crawl to dry safety. If they are lucky. I was lucky, wasn't I?'

She started moving back, away from the river, with the three remaining from the group falling in with her. Phil followed unwillingly, abandoning any hope of a sale, but needing the station himself.

'Is it a friendly area?' asked the woman of the couple.

'You know,' Maggie said, 'I think it's like most ordinary places. If you make the effort people will appreciate it, and make you welcome. It's a little like going on holiday to a foreign country. I suppose it must feel that way, if you're not used to Muslim communities, My sailor granddad back then was a Muslim, nearly all of them were. Apparently some of them tried to convert the Christians, and vice versa. And that was, what, a hundred and fifty years ago? Ahmed will know more about that. I went to school with him, and I seem to remember he knows a lot.'

They were back at the market again, and Ahmed was by a bench with three similarly dressed men.

'Hey, Ahmed, I was telling these people about the Muslim sailors back in the day. You know all about that, don't you?'

'Yes, that was a long time ago, but even earlier, at the very beginning of the nineteenth century, in this area, there was a procession of four hundred smartly dressed Muslims celebrating the Assumption of Mohammed into Paradise. Can you imagine that?'

'Well, it's been very nice to meet you,' said the single woman, echoed by the couple, 'it really seems an interesting area. But I don't think I can afford what I want round here.'

'Nor can we,' laughed Maggie, 'and we're only renting. Two hundred grand? I'm pressed to find two hundred a month. Bye. Bye,' she waved then turned to Ahmed.

'I see you every day,' said Ahmed, 'but we have never spoken before. I wonder why we are so reluctant.'

'Well, you'll remember Maggie in future,' she said, 'and I won't give your bench a wide berth.'

'Oh, our elders' meeting place by the market? They don't bite, you know.'

Phil, meanwhile, remembered one final failure to add to the rest. He had arranged for deliveries from Harvey Nichols and Waitrose to be made to two flats on one of the estates, at Rich & Strange's expense, to impress the group. Neither van had turned up. He looked at his text messages. An incident at Aldgate had prevented the deliveries being made at the time requested. Another attempt would be made at 6.30 p.m. Great. As he put his phone away he almost tripped over the small man with the alphabet fixation.

'Ah! You're still here, good! I've put the Queens on hold – a man on the train said there was a bust of Shadwell down by the Basin – can you tell me where it is?'

WAPPING

The Beetle
Ellie Stewart

After you left, the world changed colour.

I know: you'd tossed me back and forth for years. But when you finally ended it – sick of the crying and begging, you said – the air turned blue and black around me. I stumbled in the dim light. Like a bruised fruit, I became unpleasant to taste. The years folded over, and I met another, and another. I lay in their arms and allowed them to enter. For you had broken all my limbs; it took me an age to mend them. They fused crooked and strange, but in the long hours I started to see light. I saw the opportunity to grow a new life, off the crippled back of the old one. Your generosity had been marvellous, really: you'd broken me, and given me the chance to rebuild. And I never had the heart to throw that one picture of you and me away. The one where we were drunk, and our eyes were wide, and smoke filled the background air.

Wapping Station is the place where you promised to meet me again.

I fell for you under a black umbrella, when the shoppers ran to catch the bus in Leeds. You had spent the whole day trying to kiss me. At 4 p.m., outside a discount clothing store, I let you.

Today it rains too, in the morning. The streets are wet. I walk the cobble lines and raise my head to the wind, and watch: these wharves, the curled white plaster on the windows, the street lamps snuffed. The air is bare. The Thames moves beside me, seeing the sky with her darkened eyes.

It has taken me two hours to get here from Kent. But I have always come to you. I remember: you had found a bright blonde girl who you took upstairs that night, after lines of cocaine, as I sat on the sofa with your friends – the room, their brains, thick and hazy with pot. We all sat in the foul living room and heard you fucking her in your bedroom.

But that was years ago. Forgiveness washes most of it away.

I watch the water spill into the drains.

A small park stands to the right of the street on the way to the station. The damp greenery of the tall trees looks peaceful.

I step beyond the wall for a moment, to wander on the path.

It is a graveyard. I see the stones rising and falling in the grass, at different stages of collapse. In the centre stands a stone crypt, the inscriptions faded by wind and rain and the words grown over with yellow bracken. I run my fingers over the worn rock. I can make out numbers, barely. Sometime in the nineteenth century – a man and his wife.

At least this grave is passed by daily, by businessmen and dog walkers. But what of those graves, over there?

The gravestones that stand propped up against the high brick wall that surrounds the park. They have been moved: the bodies no longer lie underneath. Years ago the developers came and decided to build over the dead – yet they kept the stones, out of respect. Or superstition.

They stand like a lonely family, some a century and a half old, some a little younger. The names and dates are worn, but some can be read. There: a ten-year-old boy who died in 1873; there a devoted wife and mother who departed this world in 1897.

Who was the last person to visit them?

I watch them for a while. The rainwater drips off the leaves and patters lightly on the ground.

Then I see a beetle on the path.

He is black, an inch long and on his back. His legs wave slowly in the air, as if he has half given up already. I crouch down and turn him over with my finger. His back is a black shell, dark like a pupil. He waits for a moment. I wait too. Then he sets off along the path.

What compels me to follow the beetle? Past the forgotten graves, past the crypt and through the park. He walks with such purpose, and such grace. His smallness is a virtue; his steady speed a craft.

I follow him out of the gate, and onto the cobbled streets. His feelers reach ahead of him, like long black eyes. I feel my way along the pavement with him, and I have long black eyes.

We turn and head down the street in the shadows of the wharves. Once clanging with the trade on the Thames, now they are silent: they have become aspirational apartments, that neither man nor woman enters or leaves. The beetle's feet echo as we pass between the buildings. They watch us in disdain. We carry on our way.

Now we pass the place where the house was ripped away: the end of the terrace gapes wide and is only rough grass and a broken wire fence, and the many-windowed Georgian mansions rise up beyond. Its spare light passes, and we are in the narrow streets and the wharf shadows again.

Occasionally the beetle trips and I hold my breath and worry that he'll fall on his back again. But up he gets, each time, and carries on, with greater purpose, to wherever beetles go. His home, his beetle wife, a beetle boat that leaves the river at noon to take him to the continent where better dreams may come?

The beetle veers suddenly away as a shadow blocks the sun – but then is crushed, in an instant, by another one.

The shoe swivels, and I hear the crunch of beetle bones on paving stones.

I look up, and you are there.

'Hello,' you say, and kiss me on the cheek.

'Hello,' I say and, in a daze, let you kiss me.

We walk, back the way we came. I leave the crushed body of the beetle outside Wapping Station.

At least you were quick with it.

You are less quick with me.

You touch my arms and look into my eyes, and tell me how much you've missed me. And we laugh: it's strange, but we do laugh, and I find myself forgetting, forgetting that cataclysmic pain and the tears and the nights and the bottle and running blood: it's all water running into drains. And your bright eyes and long fingers seem to dance. We linger in the Town of Ramsgate pub 'til the bell for last orders rings.

We go dancing down the cobbled streets of Wapping and our laughter echoes in the air. We go in through one of those doors at the old wharves, and take the lift to the top floor. The lift hums, and is airless.

Your apartment has lights in the ceiling, and your fridge is full of Champagne. Your bed is big; the bed linen is white; the covers fold around my head as you push yourself in.

There is no time moving in your apartment.

I turn my head and see a picture of your girlfriend with blonde hair smiling in a silver frame.

I turn away. The window is open and the Thames moves by, outside.

I find the quiet of the air, with my long black eyes.

ROTHERHITHE

A Place of Departures
Cherry Potts

Rotherhithe is a place of departures, of ghosts hesitating on the threshold of a new life, a new world, an afterlife.

Through this alley…

From here you might have seen Captain Kidd dance at the end of the hangman's rope across the water at Wapping, or felt the brush of Fear Brewster's dress as, clutching her sister Patience's hand, she stepped onto the deck of the *Anne*; or perhaps you might have heard Mary Read cursing her family as she set out for the Caribbean and an un-looked-for life of criminality and female fellowship.

Fear, named for her mother's dread, has known nothing but hiding and running and whispering. She is seventeen now, on the cusp of womanhood, and this is the final flit. She knows that she is putting danger behind her; the future holds nothing but hope. She whispers, as her reaching toe touches the deck and she lifts her trailing foot from the earth of Europe for the last time, a promise to herself.

When I reach the New World, I shall have a new name.

I shall be Fearless Brewster.

There was a new name: within two years Fear had married Isaac Allerton. Within another seven years she was dead.

Is that so, sir? Amsterdam – are you sure? Wiki*pedia*? You can't believe everything you read on the internet now, can you? This is the very wharf that the *Mayflower* left from on that momentous journey. I expect some of the timbers are the very same. Of course the pub was just called *The Ship* back then. Shall we call in for a glass? No, madam, not the original building, sadly.

Round this corner…

From here you might have been the first person to walk under the river, shoulder to shoulder with Brunel, or here, picked up a diamond ring from among the soil and refuse of a city all but overwhelmed with its own sewage: cholera and typhoid constant companions to the mudlarks in search of treasure along the low tide mud.

Young Brunel nearly drowned in his tunnel.

He notices the rats first, the usual scuffling snuffling dart transformed into a concerted dash, and so many at a time. The men have told him about this, laughing, *like a sinking ship*, but no-one is laughing now. As the water plumes almost into his face and the mud beyond bellies in threat, they throw down tools, leap off the scaffolds and run, already splashing, through water that is rising fast.

Brunel swerves into the companion tunnel calling to the others to follow: there is no water here, yet. He stops for a moment to marvel at the sheer force of noise that the torrent makes, *cannon have nothing on it*, he says later. His feet are swept from under him, and he falls, momentarily submerged, eye to eye with a swimming rat. He can see no panic in the rat's gaze; it swims with purpose and energy. His foot is caught in the debris, he kicks, kicks again … cannot get free; the water around his ears, not quite swimming yet, but soon he will have to. He writhes and sees the rat skip neatly up the lip of the stair. *Here,* he yells, frantic for the unseen men around him, *here*! He forces himself up and into the shaft. He barks elbows and knees as he twists and crawls up to the air, accompanied by busy rats that run over his arms and ahead, used to escaping, complex maps of London's underworld stored in their clever little brains. And then the wave takes him and smashes him into the wall, and there is no swimming, no climbing, only confusion and choking – and in his mind, the teeth of a gigantic rat haul him free of the sucking Thames, but it is a hand wound into his collar that drags him out of the water.

He will tell this story often as time goes on, joking that if he hadn't been quick on his feet, there'd have been no Clifton Suspension Bridge, and certainly no Great Eastern. He doesn't mention Ball and Collins, the two men with him on that scaffold, nor the other four who drowned with them, nor the rats, paddling calmly at his shoulder.

Down these steps...

So the tunnel where Brunel nearly drowned runs from below here. Mind your head there. No, no; nothing to be worried about, it's only flooded five times; there's no danger now. Though the tunnel is quite close to the surface, can't call it surface when there's water – the river bed then. Just think, when your tube is zipping through on the way to Wapping there's only a few feet between you and the Thames. Marvellous technologists, those Vict... How *many* feet? I'm afraid I don't know exactly, young man; it would depend on how much mud has settled since, surely. It can't have been more than three or four at the time, and briefly of course, none at all.

Along this passageway...

This is a place of the unburied: tarred bodies rising in chains out of the receding tide, grinning reminders to passing ships of the fate of pirates – not all rum, sex and fancy clothes after all; and the resurrection men making midnight contracts with the anatomists of Guy's Hospital. There's quite a few of my ancestors buried in that boneyard, at least I hope they are – a final resting place in the churchyard of St Mary's is not quite final, nor so restful. And the jumpers, of course; dragged out by the watermen, when dying seems simpler than living. The dead have a way of rising, around here, a bit early for judgement day.

So here you are, indecisive, on the bank of the river. It's

quite a drop, these days. The water is cleaner than it has ever been, allegedly; depending on how far back you go. It won't be the filth that kills you these days. *Are you sure it's as bad as that lovey?* The kind voice of the copper, leaning confidentially at your elbow, considering the drop with you. Is it as bad as that?

Away you come, that's it; through this alley, we're not afraid of Captain Kidd, are we? Now around this corner, that's it, yes… Down these steps – there – nothing to be afraid of.

Mary Read dresses as a man, smokes and swears. She used to call herself by her dead brother's name, used to fight for *Kinge and Countrie* all round Europe. But peace and boredom intervene, and at last the death of her man nags her into returning to sea.

The relief of britches and a salt wind, she confides to her shipmate, as they rest between battles, no longer on the side of the King. And the shipmate plants a kiss on her lips, and pulls Mary's hand within his jerkin to feel the soft curve of a womanly breast. Ann Bonney claims that she had no idea Mary was a woman the first time she kissed her.

My eye, Mary declares, lighting her long clay pipe.

But despite that kiss and fumble and perhaps more that neither will admit to, Mary escapes the hangman's noose by dying of a child-bed fever before they have a chance to string her up.

Me, sir? I'm no-one interesting, lived here all my life, man and boy. My Dad was a docker, back when these warehouses had wares in them. This used to be Sailortown, all along here, a company town, every building and every soul owned by the East India Company. More languages than the Tower of Babel my old granddad used to say.

Almost no-one from those times still here; scattered to the four winds, as it were. For generations my family have been leaving: to Bristol with Isambard Kingdom Brunel, America with the Brewsters, the Caribbean with Mary and Ann, and on from there: Canada, Australia, Japan; some of them even went to Chingford.

Really, madam? Your father lived here in the fifties? I shouldn't wonder we're related. I jest, naturally. Your father wouldn't recognise it, not with all these new buildings, and everyone working somewhere else. This used to be where the work was. Sometimes I feel like I'm walking through a set from one of those sixties TV shows, *The Avengers*, or *Randall and Hopkirk*, that always looked like they couldn't afford to pay extras. It's so quiet here these days.

Me? Why would I leave? Where would I go? Rotherhithe is my place, it's in my blood. Redriffes have always been here, since Behemond had the neighbouring island, I shouldn't wonder. But the Redriffe family is restless, can't sit still, got to be on the move, on the water. You could say we have an affinity with water: live beside it, make our living on it or from it, travel across it – though personally I'd say I'm something of a throwback. I've more of an affinity with the foreshore. I found a gold buckle once, caught in the mud. Fifteenth century apparently – no, not valuable, not enough to retire on, anyway – it was only about an inch across. Redriffes have always been here. We were certainly here when Duke William sent his tax collectors to count heads in 1086. We were here before that, when Canute was building his canal, though as to whether we were helping dig the channel, or manning the barricades against him I can't say. But we've been leaving here for just as long, a slow trickle of Redriffes off to see the world, and die there; everyone but me.

Canute, still years away from showing his Earls the limitations of worldly power, turns and claps me on the shoulder. *Good work*, he says. Slow, maybe, but patient and determined, digging in the sticky clay. Canute asks my name. I reply, not much awed at being spoken to by the leader of the foreign invaders. I rest on my shovel a moment and consider this Canute: a man after my own heart; a man who sees water for what it is, and people for what they are, and that good dry land keeps you rooted. *Riff,* he says to me, *keep your feet dry.*

Right, ladies and gents, here we are, safe and sound and back at the Overground station. Have a safe journey, wherever you are going next.

Thank you, young sir; that is most generous, keep your feet dry, now.

CANADA WATER

No Prob at Canada Water
Anna Fodorova

Usually, the change at Canada Water went as smooth as butter. She liked the station's massive steel columns and glass tubes through which the trains glided in and out like subterranean larvae. But today the female voice informed them of a delay. The crowd remained stoic, not even a muted sigh. And already she missed Piotrek. Missed leaning against his chest, his breath warm on her hair.

'One Saturday or Sunday we'll come to see what's up there,' they promised each other every time they joined the human river spilling out of the Overground train, cascading deeper towards the Jubilee line. And every time Ewa pictured a lake: a lake so huge that it glinted like a colossal mirror, its waters surrounded by fir trees, like an eye by eyelashes. Her dad had showed her photos of such lakes from his hitchhiking days around Ontario. Or maybe it was Quebec. 'Lakes so big they could be seen from space,' he said. 'At night there're many noises; creatures moving in the dark, water lapping, but at the same time such deep, deep silence.'

Ten minutes passed and the crowd around her thickened. She waited another five, then tried to call Piotrek. No reception. With her eyes she located the exit and started her advance, apologising all along. No-one shoved into her, no-one shouted or swore like back home, some even held in their stomachs to let her pass, saying 'no problem': *no prob* for short. She and Piotrek had adopted it as their private motto. She reached the escalator and rode it to the top. As she surfaced a glass dome opened above her and she stepped into the full light.

Piotrek picked up after the first ring. 'How you feeling, *kochanie*?' she asked.

'Took the pills you left by the bed and now feel a bit woozy. But otherwise no prob. And you, kochanie?'

'I'm already in Uni,' she said, so that he wouldn't feel cheated out of their plan. 'Talk to you later, kochanie.'

She looked around. To her right stretched a vast area of shops and parking lots. In front of her rose a curious structure seemingly standing on its head. She checked her watch: plenty of time before her lecture. Now she saw the building was perched right next to the water's edge. So it represented a ship, not a monumental skip she took it to be at first. A ship stranded by a reservoir filled with dank water lapping against rough concrete slabs. On one side struggled bleak scraps of vegetation: dry reeds, bare twigs, dwindling birch trees. In the middle, a wooden jetty protruded forward with a pavilion at its tip – a viewing area of sorts. But what was here to view? When she got to the end she saw them: two swans, a flock of ducks and several black cormorants, ruffled and scraggy, huddling on a deck slimy with moss and birds' droppings; first live cormorants she had seen. She sat on a bench and shrank her vision to take in only the birds' oily plumes; patches of grass; miniature islands of mud. She blocked her ears and the sounds of the city faded away. Now all she could hear were the shrill cries of birds. Then someone blocked her view: a young man with large thick glasses in black rims, dark hair and skin.

'You okay?'

She dropped her hands from her ears. Back home she'd take him for someone to get away from pronto, a Gypsy perhaps. But here people were different, here no-one asked what you did or where you came from.

'I'm fine.' She got up and headed back towards the station. The young man walked next to her, nonchalantly swinging a nearly empty plastic bag, his trousers flopping around his legs, hood hanging between his shoulders like a creased flag. And in his half laced trainers, his toes turning comically outwards.

'You live around here?'

'No, I'm on my way to Uni. I just wanted to look around.'

'Cool,' he said and together they glanced back over the water, the outdoor equipment sport shop stretching one whole length of the reservoir and the tall crane behind, barely visible in the morning haze. They reached the building made to look like a ship. 'Can I invite you for a coffee?' The young man pushed up his specs. Like everything else on him, they seemed too big.

She checked the time and was amazed that it had moved on so fast. Once the morning lecture started they didn't let anyone in. She extended her hand. 'I'm Ewa.' And just to make everything clear, 'I live with my boyfriend Peter.' She had never skipped a lecture before, not even once, and now this hand in hers felt unfamiliar and cold.

'Piyush', said the man.

'Wow,' she said. She liked saying wow, it felt like fizz on her lips. 'It's just that in Polish you call Peter Piotrek or Piotrush. Piyush – Piotrush, sounds almost the same.'

'In Hindi Piyush means nectar,' said the young man. 'And your boyfriend's name, does it mean anything?'

'Rock,' she said. 'In Latin, not in Polish.'

'As in rock and roll?' He suggestively twisted his hips. 'Or as in,' he put on a baritone, 'he's my rock?'

'As in a mineral.' He smiled and she noticed how white his teeth were, whiter than hers or Piotrek's, white as the snow she used to put in her mouth to suck, back home. While behind his specs his eyes were so dark that his pupils blended with the rest.

In the cafeteria they sipped their cappuccinos. Piyush paid nearly four pounds and she felt a little guilty. She and Piotrek never ate out; they got their thermos flasks and sandwiches ready the night before.

'I live locally,' said Piyush, 'I only nipped out to buy marshmallows.'

She had never met a grown man buying sweets for himself, but Piyush claimed if it weren't for marshmallows he'd flunk his exams. 'They save my ass,' he said. And she said, 'normally Piotrek and I come through Canada Water earlier because Piotrek has to be on time for work and I wait in the library before my lectures start. But today Piotrek's off sick.'

'What's wrong with him?' asked Piyush.

Why talk about Piotrek's painful bouts of what the GP casually termed funny tummy? 'He hurt his back,' she said. Not really a lie because Piotrek's back often hurt, more so when he did seven-day weeks. 'He works as a scaffolder.'

'Must be strong,' said Piyush.

Like kids skiving from school, they chewed marshmallows as they circled the water. This time between the birches she spotted a sculpture: two acrobats balancing a wooden log. The notice said these were porters unloading softwood timber from ships that used to bring it from North America.

She surveyed the acres of concrete, the sprawl of shopping malls with their limitless parking spaces. 'How did the ships get here?'

'There are canals and lakes under our feet. We're walking on water,' Piyush said.

'Walking on water?!' She put mock gravity in her words; if Piyush didn't get it, it didn't bother her. She never went to church. Back home they all did, so did Piotrek. She apologised, walked a few steps ahead and called him to ask how he was. On Google it said problems with digestion are often due to nerves. Nervous stomach. She didn't expect Piotrek to be afflicted by something like this.

The phone rang for a long time and when Piotrek finally picked up she heard sounds of bombardment and screams.

'Watching a movie,' Piotrek reported, sounding a little short. 'Now it's a tense moment. And you, kochanie?'

'On a break between lectures.' Once she was back she'd explain everything.

During the next orbit she started to feel hungry. Her sandwich was easy to break in half but she also had an apple that she didn't know how to cut without a knife.

'I have knives at home,' said Piyush. 'You're welcome to come up. But if you'd rather not I understand. Totally.'

'I'd rather not,' she said, and then worried in case he felt offended. Or thought she was afraid of him. So she added, 'Must be cool. To live locally.' Saying cool curled her tongue.

'Only for another six weeks,' said Piyush. 'Then my course's done and I'm back to Hyderabad.'

They sat on a bench. She was glad she put only cream cheese and tomatoes in and not any ham. Where he came from Piyush might not be allowed meat. While they ate she told him she and Piotrek met at school and that she liked his fair head and the little knots on his arms, already there, age ten. 'I used to tell him he looked like an albino rabbit. But I knew we'd be together, I got intuition for those things,' she said. And indeed, they came to London where she enrolled to study structural engineering and Piotrek, not yet sure what direction to take, found work. Once she got her degree his turn to study would come and hers to support them.

'You're lucky,' said Piyush. 'You can do what you want.'

They took it in turns to drink lemon tea from her flask, wiping the rim before handing it over. When it came to the apple she ate her half and then passed the other half to Piyush who didn't seem to mind biting where her mouth touched it. She noticed how dusty pale his lips were and how full.

As if addicted to motion they resumed their walking. Except for few small clouds, pink as puffs of face powder, the winter sky remained clean and crisp. 'When I get back,' said

Piyush, 'I'll have to join my father's retail business rather than doing my own thing.' She refrained from probing what Piyush's 'thing' might be, in case he didn't know. She said, 'My dad left Poland nine years ago.' And, likewise, Piyush didn't ask if she knew his whereabouts.

Once more she called Piotrek. The phone rang and rang, then the voicemail kicked in. She called again.

'You woke me up,' said Piotrek. He sounded slurry so she almost didn't recognise his voice. 'Don't call anymore, kochanie, I'm going back to sleep. See you when you get back.'

'No prob, kochanie.'

'How is he?' Piyush asked.

'Better,' she said. And then she said, 'When I was a girl I used to spin on ice skates to make everything blurry like when you press a forward button to skip over some bits.'

'What bits?' he asked, pushing up his specs.

'Bits you don't want to watch,' she said and spun on the spot till blood beat in her temples like a gong. And he steadied her and she felt his chin graze her ear.

The sun began to set, lighting the walls red. They couldn't get round the whole lake in a single go as on one side the pavement was still being laid; they made detours by a housing development with balconies with folded deck chairs, stretches of storage lots and more supermarket chains, and then back by the shop windows with their exhibits of sportswear, tents and inflatable canoes. 'One day,' she told Piyush, 'Piotrek and me will go hiking in Canada.'

They stopped to lean over the metal railings. Hard railing against the softness under her ribs, she imagined Piyush must feel the same. Looking down, she noticed that a duck had got caught inside a square of mesh fencing protecting young reeds. 'How will she get out?'

'She'll find a way out,' said Piyush. 'She's a creature of the wild.'

This made her laugh. And yet she hoped he was right,

not only for the duck. By now the water had become dark like mercury and Piyush kept breathing on his fingers, rubbing them against his nose. Seeing he wasn't used to cold and how flimsy his jacket was, she grabbed his icy hand and drew it in her warm pocket. In the fading light Piyush's face took on a hue of sand but around his eyes his skin remained like dark velvet. His thick black hair seemed matted and she wondered what it would feel like were she to touch it.

With the streetlights turning on, a flood of commuters begun streaming out of the underground towards the supermarkets and Ewa thought she should go back. But then Piotrek was probably still asleep. On their way from the shops people unwrapped soft white squares of bread and threw them in the lake. There was a rush of birds. Out of nowhere a formation of brown geese swooped in, gliding lower in ever smaller circles until they hit the water, wings stretched, feet braking the speed. Ewa and Piyush watched the birds darting here and there, like brush strokes of ink. Hammering each other with their beaks, their cackles now more like the barking of dogs. The water seemed to boil. In her pocket their fingers were locked. Mist came from their mouths.

As they passed the colossal upside-down house, its windows glowed like in a transatlantic cruiser. Glass skyscrapers shot into the sky like flames. This time they didn't turn back to the lake, they walked straight along a road lined with storage lots until they reached the place where shrubs grew against a tall fence, some still hung with berries, yellow and red. They were alone. Ewa opened her padded coat and drew him in. They shivered with cold and heat, both at the same time. The white of their eyes shone as if they too were creatures of the wild. Against hers his hips felt bony and slim as a girl's. The pleasure went through her, so intense that she cried out.

She stands on a platform again. Everything is running regularly, no delays, no problems. When she gets back she knows what to say to Piotrek. That were he to ride up the steel escalators, he would find nothing but shops, car parks and a pool of murky water housing a few scruffy birds and a ship made out of concrete destined to sail nowhere. Nothing you would want to waste your Sunday on. From the tunnel blows a gust of warm wind and around her the crowd tightens and shifts forward.

SURREY QUAYS

Three Things to do in Surrey Quays
Adrian Gantlope

Kristina had told him over the phone how to get there. By the way she had spoken he knew her eyes were squeezed closed in concentration, imagining the route to him. The directions came in her breathy staccato, a foretelling of how his journey would be.

'Left out of the station entrance,' she had said, 'not far until a sort-of-small-road-kind-of-more-like-an-alley which you need to go down all the way, then through the gap-between-the-shops to cross the big street, then to the right for a bit until you get to a shop with a kind-of-old-fashioned-green-sign and some little writing in the window (if you reach the chemists you've gone too far), and then the left down another road, and sort of behind on yourself where the road curves, there is the café tucked away, right there, it has a girl's name, Maria's café, or something like that. It is painted yellow, and not far from the dock.'

She had told him to be there at 7 a.m., and not to be late.

The walk from the station was exactly how she had described it. He wasn't trusting, and had been obliged to print a map just in case. Who was to know where he might end up? But once followed, her voice in his mind as he walked, he realised she had precision, an exactness, though of a kind without compass points or street names. The café was exactly where she had said. He folded the paper into his pocket.

It was thrilling to enter her landscape. Every step he took from the station was laying a paving stone, building a path on which they both trod, fixing them permanently into the same geography. She had been so cautious until now. They had met several times, but always according to the rules, in open and well-lit spots with multiple exits, busy places where she could not become alone with him. She chose where, every time. Never far from a chain restaurant offering foods of pan-global neutrality. Usually they would take a short walk afterwards. She preferred the riverside to anywhere else in the city and, with the seriousness of a person who had adopted the city, would tell him about the history of the river and how, like an umbilicus, it had fed the growth of the city, sustained and nurtured its development before being ignored and neglected.

'Anything amazing you can imagine has come up this river,' she would say, 'and once inside it never goes back out, it is just used up or changed into something else. And what is left behind is thrown away as rubbish, and it is mainly rubbish which goes back down the river again.'

She had told him how she would like to go back in time and be the one who brings objects to the city. She would travel on a sailing ship and see the old world, and the new world, every port, every coastline. She would collect Moluccan spices, freshly picked from their shrubs, catch a Dodo. She would accompany the British army to remove the stones from the Parthenon, bring tea from China and wine from Capetown. And catch a whale to bring to be dismembered on the dock.

He would try to come early for their meetings and find a hidden spot to watch her arrival. He had worked out, even before she had told him, more-or-less where she lived. Their meetings were often in different places, but all within a certain range, he had drawn them out. They were all a twenty minute journey for her, he figured. Taking account of travel, their meal and a little walk, she would be back to her place within four hours of leaving. He had guessed domestic commitments, and was right. He had imagined a husband but asked her if she had kids to look after. In fact it was neither. She told him little about the old lady, her boss, other than she allowed her one afternoon off a week, usually Tuesdays. She could go after finishing washing up lunch as long as she was back in time to make a cold supper, the lady didn't mind a cold supper once a week.

And yesterday the old lady died, she had told him.

And she needed him to come to help her. Him!

It was getting light, and the rising sun reflected from the masts of the boats in the marina. A plume of steam rose from a houseboat, and the fried food smell from the cafe reminded him that he had not had breakfast. Even though he was much earlier than she had said, she was already there, sitting at a table nearest the window, in her coat. She looked like she hadn't slept, and her puffy eyes showed she had been crying.

'Richard,' she said, 'Thank you for coming, and in very good time too.'

'Hello Kristina,' he said, 'no problem, I'm pleased to help. I know you're sad, but don't you have even a little smile for me today?'

She held her fingers to the corners of her lips and pulled them up into a wan smile, before breaking into a real one. 'It's true, Richard. I am a bit sad, and have had a lot of things to think about since yesterday, but already I feel better for seeing you. Let's walk, there are three things I would like you to do for me. '

They walked together towards the apartment block overlooking the dock. It was secure, gated from the streets around, entrance by card only. The card was needed to enter the doorway to the apartment block, and a separate card was required to get the lift to the sixth floor.

'The old lady's children are coming later, Richard,' she told him, 'and I will have to leave here, I'm afraid. It's been nearly three years, and this is my last day. I have my two suitcases already packed, and the one of the three things that I want you to do is to help me take them to the station, later. That is if you don't mind.'

'Of course,' he said.

Considering the luxury appearance of the block, Richard was surprised by the rank odour of cat urine which hit his nostrils when Kristina opened the door. She laughed a little at his discomfort. 'Oh yes, my boss she loved her cats. She would get them from the rescue centre and let them rule in here. She would always take the ones that nobody wanted, old ones and incontinent ones, ones with cat AIDS. None of them live for very long, and of course I had to clean up after them for her, and get rid of them when they die. There is just one cat here at the moment, a little monster that you cannot even stroke because it will scratch your hands to ribbons. Don't worry; I have shut it in the bathroom so it shouldn't bother us, apart from its nasty smell.'

The sitting room was small and crammed with art objects. The limited amount of furniture, a sofa and an armchair was expensive and stylish, framed in a hard wood, and covered in a loose woven natural material, dyed in off-whites, beiges and browns. There was a fine view through a large picture window, looking east over the houseboats in the dock below and beyond to the wide river. Kristina made tea and they sat down on the sofa together, looking out.

'So you finally get to see where I live. On my last day. In fact you are my first ever visitor. First and last,' she laughed dryly. 'I have no-one in this country to see me, and now no job and no home. You know, Richard, I have never asked you about your family. Do you have one? Tell me about them.'

'Well, when we meet we talk about so many other things that are more interesting than family,' he said, 'but no, I don't have much family. I used to be married, but have no children. My parents are dead. I have a brother who lives in Surbiton, with his own family, a wife and three children who I see at Christmas, usually, though not so much now his children are growing up.

His wife doesn't like me much, I think. To tell the truth, I don't much like her either.'

'Well then, that brings me to number two,' she said.

She brought her face to his and kissed him on the lips, keeping them there for a long time. He felt her passion and her urgency. She pressed her body tightly against his, and reached her tiny hand up and slid it inside his shirt and stroked his chest. Her eyes stayed closed, but he kept his open, alternating between looking at her white-blonde hair pulled back in a tight pony tail, and watching a yellow barge being slowly pulled down the river by a tug.

'You are a good kisser, Richard,' she said after a while.

'I thought you would be. I've been waiting for this opportunity.'

They finished their tea. They watched over the river together. Another barge was being pulled down the river and a small passenger plane descended steeply to land in the City Airport. As it banked, its silver fuselage glittered in the morning sunshine.

'You see, everything comes in shiny, and it goes out in bins,' she said. 'You want to know about my request number three, Richard? Are you a good chooser?'

The old lady had known she was dying, of course. But not when it would occur. She had contracted a lingering uncertain kind of bowel cancer which progressed slowly, with periods of remission. Sometimes she had been well enough to sit and knit, to take walks, and receive visitors. Kristina told Richard that the old lady had promised her that she could take something after her death. Anything she chose to.

'Well I'm certainly not going to take the cat, Richard,' she said. 'But the children wouldn't let me take anything else, I think. There is nothing written in her will, and the children already treat me like I was some kind of thief, a gold-digger.'

She looked around. 'There are so many nice things she has

collected. I sometimes think she has been everywhere in the world. And she had such good taste, I cannot choose on my own.'

Richard couldn't have ignored the old lady's love of art. The living room was like a treasure trove, a museum in miniature. A troupe of ebony carved hunters stood on the floor, watched from the walls by grimacing tribal masks. Kristina and he walked around, looking closely at the things in the room.

'So what do you think, Richard? What should I take?'

The small framed sketch above the TV, which he first assumed was a print, looked very much like an original Picasso. Another sketch was by Peake, there was a small Magritte painting, and possibly a Miró. The deep wooden bookshelves on two of the walls were stacked with small sculptures and objects. A dog-headed boatman ferrying tiny figures in a small funeral boat could well have been from an Egyptian tomb. Stone fertility statues sat next to intricate silverware, ancient coins and engraved glass.

They were systematic, considering each one. She had spent time with all of them, and each had taken some meaning for her. He looked at her too, trying to understand from her expression what she might like most to keep. One object was a silver oyster, tiny and probably of little value, just something for a charm bracelet.

'This one intrigues me, Richard,' she said. 'It isn't like her other things.'

'You find oyster shells in middens,' he told her.

'What are middens?' she said. 'They sound interesting.'

'Old waste-dumps,' he said. 'The ones in London were often packed with shells, though none as shiny as this one. And as they say, the world's your oyster.'

'So this will be my oyster, now.' She smiled, and stretched to kiss him again.

It fitted neatly into her pocket. They walked back to the station, one hand each for a suitcase, and one for each other.

NEW CROSS

New Cross Nocturne
David Bausor

'Non-British students must be prepared to find many things to be different and/or challenging.'

Koo-Ja swiped her ticket across the yellow circle. Once again, the machine did nothing, and the gates would not open.

Koo-Ja felt her vision starting to blur.

She'd followed the instructions carefully. Arrive Heathrow, the airport crowded and smelling of sweat and cleaning solution. Catch the Piccadilly line to Green Park, then Jubilee line to Canada Water, then the Overground line to New Cross. On the Overground, the train had suddenly risen out of the earth, exposing a series of apartment blocks and warehouses crowding up against the rails. Her first glimpse of London. Everything felt both strange and familiar, like a place that you come home to in a dream.

At New Cross (step eight on her father's list), everyone got off the train. Carrying her luggage down the platform, she had seen that the tracks ended here. They ran up against a red painted stanchion and stopped like a broken promise. A minute later, she had encountered the metal gates.

Don't panic, Koo-Ja, she told herself, and stepped to the side. She watched people leaving, swiping their tickets, the barrier opening, passing through to carry on with their lives. Why did this not work for her? Did the machine somehow sense her hesitation, and refuse her ticket out of sheer spite?

Packed away in her suitcase with her admission letter was a leaflet. It was addressed to 'All Prospective Students', but Koo-Ja's family had read it together. It said: 'Non-British students must be prepared to find many things to be different and/or challenging.' Even Koo-Ja's father thought that this was good advice, and the conductor of Seoul's second finest orchestra did not take advice gladly. That was why he had given her the instructions: precise, numbered, stage by stage, explaining how to get to Surrey House, the student hall of residence on Lewisham Way. From the internet, Koo-Ja knew that 'Surrey' was an English county known for its green fields and friendly locals. She imagined Lewisham was probably like that too, and it would be good to find herself in such a place.

But she had to get there first.

She glanced around for help. There were ticket windows on the other side of the gates. Presumably there were people inside – but that was useless: if she could get to them, she would not need help. She noticed a brass plaque by one window that read: 'Runner-Up: Best Managed Station (In Difficult Circumstances) 1998.' In 1998 Koo-Ja had been four years old. She wondered what the difficult circumstances had been. Floods? Fire? Riots, maybe. She'd seen the English rioting on television. Afterwards, it had taken ages to reassure her parents that London was safe, a worthy place to study.

Koo-Ja was almost crying now. Everything about this wretched station threatened 'difficult circumstances': its obstinate gates, the smell of dust and burning rubber, the cracked and dirty tiles that lined the floor and the walls. Koo-Ja wished that she was home in Seoul again, watching the English burn their red double-decker buses.

'All right, miss?' A man in a blue uniform was at her elbow. She tried to smile.

'Help yes,' she said, slowly and clearly as she had been taught. 'I go to university.'

She pointed south, down where she imagined the Goldsmiths campus was: grand stone buildings and ivy-covered cloisters the way she'd seen in a documentary about English universities on KBS once.

'Music,' she said, and held up the cello case.

'OK,' said the guard. Koo-Ja noticed that he was older, about her father's age. He had kind brown eyes, and he seemed to be expecting something else.

'Help yes,' she said again, waving at the barriers.

The guard glanced down at her ticket.

'Seems okay. Just go through, love, or do you want to use the luggage gate?'

She didn't understand. He spoke too quickly.

Koo-Ja decided to show him exactly what the problem was. She swiped the ticket against the yellow circle, once again nothing happened.

'Bless you, that's only for Oyster cards.'

He reached over and took the ticket, and slipped it into a slot she hadn't noticed. The machine sucked it in, and the gates clunked open.

She hesitated, then stepped forward. Another step, and another, and then she was through. Simple.

'That's right, love, off you go.' Then he was passing her luggage to her over the top of the barrier.

'Kam-sa-ham-ni-da,' she said, forgetting.

Outside, it was dusk. The street lights cast a yellow glow that made Koo-Ja think of hospitals. Over the road, she noticed a basement café offering 'ALLDAY BREAK-FAST'. She smiled: it was as if she had come to a place where time had ceased to matter. Suddenly, she felt very homesick. Her last meal at home had been breakfast – her mother's juk, the rice grains fat and sweet. Since then, she'd travelled for more than fifteen hours, but somehow arriving here it was still time for breakfast.

Koo-Ja turned right (step nine), and discovered a broad

highway, cars oozing slowly into the distance as far as she could see. Step ten, New Cross Road. She crossed at the traffic lights, and stopped to get her bearings. She leaned the cello case against a wall the colour of burnt mustard. Large metal letters along the top of the building spelled out 'Amersham Arms'. Underneath a dirty white banner said 'Live Music Saturday' in big letters, and underneath in much smaller letters, 'Jumble Sale Wednesday'. Whenever the double doors on the corner opened, an aroma of stale alcohol wafted out: a flat, bitter smell that tasted like disappointment. This must be one of the famous English pubs she'd heard about, where everyone drank warm beer and roasted chestnuts while their dogs lay asleep in front of the fire.

Turning the corner onto Amersham Way (step eleven), she discovered several tables. They seemed to be piled with rubbish – books, toys, kitchen implements, and an enormous stuffed lion with dirty yellow fur. One of the tables had several milk crates filled with old vinyl records.

Koo-Ja loved records.

When she was young, she'd played them on her mother's portable record player – a boxy thing of pink plastic that Koo-Ja couldn't break, no matter how many times it accidentally got dropped on her bedroom floor. She had listened to music for hours, really heard it for the first time – the Beatles, Mozart's piano concertos, the haunting cadences of Gregorian chants. Her mother loved Mozart; her father had preferred Chopin. Koo-Ja had collected the pop music herself, carefully stacking all the albums in alphabetical order.

The man behind the table had a narrow, clever face that made him look like a rodent. He was arguing with a boy about Koo-Ja's age.

'No refunds, mate,' he said.

'But this isn't the Beatles!' argued the boy, holding up an album Koo-Ja recognized as Abbey Road. 'This is the Magic Roundabout's 1973 Christmas album!'

A girl pushed past Koo-Ja. The girl had angel wings attached to her back with two strips of elastic. The left one was slightly tattered as if she had once flown too close to a flame.

'Leave it, Henry,' said the girl.

She pulled at the boy's arm, and grudgingly he went with her.

Rodent-face suddenly switched his attention to Koo-Ja.

'Hello, my dear,' he said smoothly. 'What choo need?'

Koo-Ja ducked her head and began to flip through the records in the nearest milk crate. She passed over young men in tartan on the Bay City Rollers' 'Greatest Hits', horror show makeup for Kiss' 'Love Gun', the New York Philharmonic playing the 1812 Overture.

'They're good records, my lovely,' said Rodent. 'Yours for only a pound.'

Koo-Ja pulled a record out of the box. Soviet State Radio Symphony Orchestra: 'Live at the Royal Albert Hall'. There was a black and white photograph of the orchestra playing their instruments: the men serious and solid in badly fitting suits, and a single woman sitting ready at a harp, her hands flat against her thighs.

She knew this record: she had her own copy. The first movement of Shostakovich's Violin Concerto No 1 was one of her favourites: a gentle, sombre nocturne, the notes swaying with graceful beauty. She had cried the first time she heard it. Had it been then she decided to become a musician? No, it couldn't have been – she had probably been six or seven when she first played that record. But holding the thin cardboard sleeve on an alien street she felt as if it might have been the unwitting beginning of something that was only now fully unfolding.

Koo-Ja weighed the album in her hands. It felt incredibly light and flimsy, as if it could suddenly glide off into the dark-blue twilight like a bat. Suddenly she remembered Henry and the girl with the angel's wings, and pressed her thumbs together. There was a record in there, she could feel it, but what guarantees did she have that it was the Soviet State Radio Symphony Orchestra?

'I look to see scratches?' she asked.

'Sorry love. No touching the merchandise. Can't risk damaging the goods, you see. Records is awful bad for scratches.'

Rodent reached to take the album away from her.

She didn't understand most of what he was saying, and for a moment, she was tempted to just let it go. It had been years since she'd heard that record. She'd played it until it was badly scratched – a few seconds of music, and then SCCRRIIP! It had been her father's record too, something that he had bought her mother years ago, (or her mother had bought him?), but surprisingly he had not been angry.

'Things break sometimes, Koo-Ja,' he'd said, tracing the worst of the scratches with his finger. One ran all the way from the outer circumference to the centre, as if the black surface had been slashed with a knife. She couldn't remember how that had happened. 'Sometimes they can be fixed,' and he lowered the record to the turntable, and pressed the button to make it play. 'And sometimes they can't,' he'd said, as they had listened together to the interplay of orchestra and static, beauty and cacophony alternating like day and night.

'Let me put it back for you, my dear,' said Rodent. 'You probably don't even have a record player to put it on. You look more like the iPod generation to me.'

This Rodent was not right, thought Koo-Ja. She had a record player. It was under her bed in Seoul. Now she remembered how she had scratched the record. She had been hurrying to put it away and had missed the sleeve. The record fell to the floor and rolled until it clattered to a stop against the skirting board. 'You are so clumsy, Koo-Ja,' chided her mother, picking up the fallen record. Then her mother had tucked her into bed, and Koo-Ja had slept soundly, not knowing her record now had a scar from one side to the other.

'You will find many things to be different and/or

challenging,' she thought. But here was something familiar, and not just that: redemption, a chance to regain what was lost. If the record would not play, she would pin the album cover to her wall. When her parents came to visit, they would surely notice: they could laugh about it together, a journey that needed no written instructions at all.

How often can we purchase such riches for a pound?

'Sorry?' said Rodent warily.

She realised that she had spoken aloud, and in Korean. She fumbled one of the unfamiliar golden coins from her pocket.

'I take the record,' she said. 'Please.'

'Enjoy,' he said. 'Nice bit of music that.'

She turned away and pulled the record out of its paper sleeve. Her heart sank.

It wasn't the Soviet State Radio Symphony Orchestra live at the Albert Hall. Instead, the label read 'Brand new psychobilly! The Bastards Out Of Canada Water debut EP – 'Wanking in Wapping'.'

Koo-Ja held up the album cover in one hand and the record in the other.

'This is not Soviet State Radio Symphony Orchestra,' she said slowly and clearly. 'This is not Albert Hall.'

'Sorry love,' replied Rodent. 'All sales are final.' He peered at the record. 'That's a great EP though – I saw those Bastards play at the Albany in Deptford once.'

She didn't understand what he was talking about. The record was music certainly, but she guessed it was not the kind you could hear at the Albert Hall. For a moment, she wanted to smash the record on the table's edge, see its shiny surface shatter into ebony shards.

Life cheated you sometimes. That was all there was to it.

It sounded like her father's voice, but not quite: younger and kinder somehow. Koo-Ja put the record carefully back in the cardboard sleeve.

'I do not complain,' she said to Rodent, conscious of his eyes upon her.

'No refunds,' replied Rodent loudly. She realised Rodent was staring over her shoulder. 'I thought I told you to fuck off already.'

It was Henry, returned with his angel in tow.

She moved aside quickly when Rodent came out from behind his table. Then there was some shoving, and then Rodent was pushing the shouting boy along the street. The angel girl trailed behind, screeching something unintelligible.

Koo-Ja held her record tightly. It felt precious, like a strange pearl she had saved from a difficult sea. She did not know who these Bastards were, or what their connection to Canada Water might be. She realised that she had passed through it on the train. She remembered only a dimly lit pause in the darkness between the tunnels.

A jet droned low overhead. Koo-Ja felt more tired than she had ever been. She thought it would be wonderful to climb into a warm bed with clean sheets, and sleep and sleep and sleep. Surrey House was the last step on her printed list of instructions, and she was almost there. She tucked the record under her arm. Time to go.

When she looked down, her suitcase was there but the cello was gone.

NEW CROSS GATE

Yellow Tulips
Rob Walton

I have been chased in that street. That street outside that station. I have been threatened in that street. That street outside that station. I have been given flowers in that street. That street outside that station. I have kissed, made up, fallen out, fallen out of love; in that street outside that station.

I have lived in the area for only a few months, but that is long enough for hundreds of visits to the station, though if truth be told, and I have been known to tell it, I keep no tally. I have no diary, no journal, no Paperchase notebook with marginalia. I have only memories, and those perhaps invented. Maybe there haven't been hundreds of visits, departures, arrivals. Maybe it only seems like hundreds. But I have surely been there sometimes. There with him and there with her.

I have surely locked my cycle hundreds of times. Have had hundreds of coffees, but measured nothing with the spindly plastic stirrers.

Hundreds. I have hundreds of memories of the station, hundreds of thoughts, ideas, flights of fancy. And so many journeys. Some of them in my head, some of them on train tracks. Some of them with her and some of them with him. And some, of course, alone. That is, alone with my thoughts, which maybe isn't alone at all. On reflection – reflection! – that is certainly not alone.

I don't know why John and Alex had such a profound

effect on my life. I met them in the pub across the road from the station. A mid-week evening in July, all three of us looking somehow related in our pale short-sleeved shirts, pale shorts and dark plimsolls with no socks. I think they asked if they could join me at my table. I think that was the way it went. John spoke first. Alex mostly smiled.

On a Tuesday John gave me flowers. They had been given to him by Alex. It was complicated. It was symptomatic. It was, at times, messy. There was a lot of love involved one way or the other, but it was messy. Complicated and messy. Some things have to be messy but this was – ah! – this was – oh! – needlessly so. I was given the flowers on New Cross Road, on the way to the train station, and placed them in the bin on the approach. They were surely bought across the way there, next to the pub, the pub with the students. At the end of the day they were still there, still wrapped in cellophane. That's the flowers, by the way, not the students. Perhaps the students could be wrapped in cellophane for a project, but the ones I saw looked wrapped up in themselves, sometimes each other, never with me. Though once I'd invited such affections, such contact.

And the flowers in the cellophane in the bin? I'd spent that Tuesday thinking and things had changed, at least in my head. I got off the train at about five, took them out of the bin, took them home, took the blue vase Alex had bought me. (More complications: John had an identical one. Only his was still in the bubble wrap, in the cupboard under the television. I'd been house-sitting and saw it as an opportunity to confirm a few things.) I poured an inch of lemonade in the bottom of the vase, before topping it up with lukewarm water. We all have our ways with cut flowers, foibles even, and this was mine.

They were tulips. You wouldn't expect them to keep for a whole day. Not in a bin. Not tulips. Not yellow tulips.

I don't only have cut flower foibles of course. I have counting-in-my-head foibles. I have touching coping stone ways.

I have ways of waiting for friends at the train station, but they have changed over the years. It was once the quick crossword in the broadsheet which became something called a Berliner, but now it's the word games on the mobile phone. I don't like myself for it, but it's what I do.

When I'm waiting there. When I'm meeting them there. Him there. Her there. You may choose whether to believe me when I say I meet others there, of course, but it was usually him or her. And sometimes I waited, wait, for no-one, just wait. Only not just wait. Wait and see.

The arrangements were usually made by text, though I had no objection to making phone calls. They had busy lives, and I acknowledged that, didn't want to take up too much of their time. I was not a fan of shorthand – you may have gathered as much, may have worked that one out all by yourself, on your own – I never liked the text speak. But for the meetings I would tap out 'NXG? 7:30? X'. And the reply would come back 'NXG it is'. Then I would think, did they read the bit about 7:30? I wasn't only sorting out the place. I'd made reference to the time. Did I need to sort out the time as well? As I said, they had busy lives; I had more time to dwell on such matters.

To a point we all thought alike about the meeting place and its aptness. We could meet there, turn our backs on the train station and go to the pub, to a bar, for a meal. Or we could take the train to his favourite stop – we'd be going north – and live dangerously. Or take the train to her favourite stop – we'd be going south – and live yet more dangerously. We all liked the flexibility, fluidity. We relished the options, savoured the possibilities. For a long time we'd toss a coin to work out our direction. Then we'd roll a dice to work out our destination station. We obviously never got further than six stations away in either direction. Ah! Let's walk up the road to the gallery again! Anyone for Anerley? At one point Alex started working as a classroom assistant and brought something called a nine-sided or nine-faced dice. Strangely it never came up with a number higher than 6 (which was actually 6, so it didn't get mixed up with 9).

In many aspects of our lives we'd taken out the choices but in this at least they remained.

There was a day when Alex chose. She was late, uncharacteristically so. I spent some time leaning on the black railings, moving my phone along them. I realised after three of four of these movements that, even though my phone was protected by a cheap black rubber case (ah, the smell of cheap rubber) which I had bought via the internet, this was not guaranteed to protect it from this sort of treatment. I stopped. I went through my pockets, placing used sweet wrappers in the blue bin liners in the bins. Why blue? I wondered. It made me think of a hospital for some reason, perhaps to do with gowns and masks. No, not a hospital – a show house: where you wear those blue plastic over-shoes. I imagined I was in a show house there on the pavement. I couldn't sustain it for long. I moved to the doorway to smoke, lighting my second cigarette directly from the first. I think that was the first time I had ever done that. The first cigarette I stubbed in the designated place to the right of the station doorway and the second I stubbed out to the left. I was aware that my behaviour wasn't quite normal, but Alex was unusually late and there was something else, a sense of being almost imperceptibly nudged. At one point as I stared at the bus stop across the road I imagined someone holding my chin and pointing my face up the street, willing me to see something I was obviously not catching of my own free will.

I was playing something called Word Mole on my phone when she approached. Finding letters to make words for points. *Tomorrow. Never. Maybe. Chance.* She seemed unusually determined and focused. This was a daytime meeting. A weekend; a Saturday. To me Saturday was quite like Tuesday or Thursday but for Alex – you know how busy she was – it was very different. She had to make the most of it, bend it to her will, her wiles, her ways.

When I got back, without Alex, I had no charge on my phone. I had to use one of the public call boxes across the road, next to the pub. I phoned John. It felt strange. I hadn't been in a phone booth since childhood, but I was pleased it was there. I decided I liked it and might try to use it again, but knew this was some feeble thinking, I knew it wouldn't happen. It was the drink talking without the drink being taken. It was words in my head, messy thoughts. It was some sort of covering up for messy thoughts about Alex and John.

It is possible to live in a city, a town, a village, an area of a city for a short time and make new friends, close friends, have altogether deeper relationships. Without the shared past or common references you can dive in to the here and now, establish a new sort of relationship, one you haven't tried before. Do all the things you didn't do in the other places you lived. Then move on and become a new you, or be one of the other yous in another new place.

Of course these relationships can fade quickly. Perhaps someone moves away, relocates with work, relocates with feelings, shifts emotionally. Some of these relationships snap quickly and you never find out why, or you don't want to find out why. People come in and out of our lives. Some we let go, some we try to cling on to.

I went to the shop John had once called his personal house clearance place, further up the road. This was the place which sold bric-a-brac, antiques, second-hand bits and pieces, pre-loved this and pre-loved that. It did, in truth, look as though much of the stuff could be found in John's flat. I bought a mirror, which was much too big for me to comfortably carry. So I did some uncomfortable carrying. All the way back to mine where I put it up, then and there. I stuck a picture of Alex on the mirror, took a pen and copied her features on to the mirror. The following week I contacted a portrait painter who painted Alex on one half of the mirror. I persuaded John to pay for it. I placed a picture of John on the wall behind. He always looked on, in miniature, when I looked in the mirror with my Alex next to me.

Sometimes, after looking in the mirror, after quickly reflecting, I think it is time to move on and I head to the station. I walk to the pub and have a drink. Sometimes I go up to strangers and ask if I may join them. Then I go to the flower shop next door to buy flowers or a plant. I head across the road and begin to wait. I no longer smoke, no longer play games on my phone. I look at the train times and the information boards outside the station and I walk up and down next to those black railings. I circumnavigate the bins and I wait. I wait for Alex, for someone, knowing the pleasure is all in the waiting.

BROCKLEY

How to Grow Old in Brockley
Rosalind Stopps

Don't look back.

Don't remember how things were, only how they are and might be. When you see a young woman spit on a pavement, tut and raise your eyebrows but only slightly, so that there is always a question about what you might mean.

Go to a cafe with a tasteful decor, the one near to the station, and keep company with a cappuccino as if you are waiting to go somewhere else. Read an interesting book, one by somebody famous.

Fill your time usefully.

Watch from behind your book. As he walks into the cafe you think of that line from an old song, the one where he walks into the party like he was walking onto a yacht. The line makes you smile and you wish that you could share the joke or even just hum it a bit but you keep quiet and keep your eyes down like a Resistance spy, even when he comes over. He sits at your table and pulls out a copy of the Guardian.

You wish that you had a matching copy so that you could say, 'snap'.

Eyes down, keep reading. Take a sip, careful not to get the froth on your lip, glance up and check out how old he is.

Make a tick list.

Grey hair – tick.

Balding – tick.

Nice eyes – difficult to tell when he is engrossed in the foreign news pages. Foreign news? Put a tick by intelligent.

Eyes down, keep reading your book – maybe by Martin Amis or Julian Barnes.

Try to think of opening lines, nothing to do with star signs, weather or trains. Discard them. Jump slightly when he says, 'the coffee's good in here, isn't it?' and bite down on an impulse to confess that you prefer Starbucks.

Starbucks indeed. You have politics – South East London leftover politics – so you nod politely, lost for words.

He goes back to reading about the Greek economy and you pinch yourself under the table. The twenty-year-old you would not have let such an opportunity go by, and you try to summon her up like a cappuccino genie. You can almost see her, hair darker than dye and full of faith in herself. In a fit of uncharacteristic whimsy, and still keeping your eyes on Mr Barnes's *Sense of an Ending*, you try to commune with Young You, ask her what to do. She looks thoughtful in her wispy way. She hovers over the table and you are surprised for a moment that Grey Bald Intelligent Man does not seem to notice her rising from a puddle of spilt coffee.

'Talk to him, you daft old woman,' she says and you smile.

He looks up, catches the smile and returns one of his in exchange. Young You wisps off into the cafe ceiling.

'Is the book funny?' he asks. You say that it is anything but.

It is a middle class, middle-aged exchange but it is yours.

It's a beginning.

During the next phase, see him twice a week. He is a thoughtful man and a good companion, bringing novels you do not want to read and chocolates you do not want to eat.

Give the chocolates to your husband, pretending that they were a gift from colleagues at work.

'Thanks,' he says, 'I'll save you from yourself, shall I?'

You are not even tempted by the coffee ones. Watch your

waistline shrink and try on some jeans from twenty years ago.

Grey Man's name is Graham, which sometimes makes you laugh.

Never explain the joke to him.

Never suggest that you meet more frequently.

Never ask probing questions.

Watch *Brief Encounter* with your husband and cry a lot while you make the tea. Pretend that you haven't noticed that he is pretending not to notice.

It's an affair, perhaps not an affair of the heart, more an affair of the memory. An old people's affair using the same battered rule book.

Walk around Brockley together while your husband watches football or fusses over the garden. Point out blossoms. Get the train up to London and ride on the Eye like a pair of wrinkled teens. Swap stories of music and travel and missed opportunities, and only start on what could have been after a glass or two of wine when your husband is away visiting his sister.

Be impressed by his wife. Of the four of you, she is the only one still working – her expertise in skin grafting so much in demand that she has been unable to retire. Imagine her, day after day slicing and stitching, grafting and grating, tired but important. Google her and try not to feel triumphant when an ordinary looking woman stares back at you from a thumbnail photograph.

Introduce skin grafting into your conversation whenever you are not with Graham, and familiarise yourself with some of the basic processes.

Spend a long time in front of the mirror, wondering if you could graft a young face onto an old one.

Make private jokes that only Graham understands, and listen to old singers in minor keys singing of lost loves.

'The thing is,' he says over coffee in the cafe you both call 'your' cafe.

'The thing is, I'm not sure where this is going.' He looks so earnest, Guardian reading and the Greek troubles forgotten in his new angst.

'This?' you say, playing for time, 'this coffee?' and you hold up a cup, playfully, pretending that you don't know what he means. You're just stalling for time, you know exactly what he means and you could have written the script yourself.

He smiles, and in the smile you can see the worst thing. Pity.

'You started it,' you want to shout but that would be undignified.

Make a quick note of the fact that dignity never came into it until you reached fifty but now it seems to be everything.

'That's fine,' you say at last with an attempt at an ironic shrug, 'no hard feelings,' although the feelings you have are as hard as concrete, as hard as advanced mathematics. But it's nearly a grown-up response and it takes him by surprise.

'Oh Ginnie,' he says and already your name sounds wrong in his mouth, as if it comes from an unfamiliar language where clicks are used instead of consonants, 'what happened?'

Stop drinking in cafes or looking in mirrors.

Help your husband in the garden.

Plan little treats, weekends away and suppers with home-made puddings.

Walk around Brockley with your head down, remembering.

Pretend not to notice your husband pretending not to notice you crying sometimes, over a sad story in the paper or when the apple tree dies, the one that your husband was hoping to graft next winter.

HONOR OAK PARK

Carrot Cake
Paula Read

'Why are my Jockeys blue?'

The roar hit Clara's ears as she was jamming the leg of five-year-old Lucia into a Wellington boot. Clara breathed. The dog started to bark at the back door – continued to bark at the back door. Anthony burst into the room waving his underpants.

'What is this?' he shouted as Clara shoved Lucia's other sturdy leg into the other boot.

Clara breathed again. She wasn't going to respond. Let Anthony yell. Wouldn't take long before he would deflate like a balloon with a pin stuck in it. Anyway, blue was an improvement. Anthony's attachment to white underwear always seemed so self-righteous, so typical of his American approach. White Jockeys – the symbol of American manhood.

'Clara, why you gotta mix up the laundry?'

The dog's barking had become more insistent, in rhythm with Clara's breathing. Both Lucia's legs were tucked tightly into her boots. Clara stood up, let the dog in. Bruce lumbered past her to his bowl, leaving a trail of mud and wet, and ate last night's remnants with the gusto of a man on death row having his last supper. Lucia was toppled in the dog's wake, but rolled over onto her knees, uncomplainingly, to hoist herself up.

'Bruce!' was all Clara could holler before kissing Lucia and brushing her down.

Anthony continued to wave his pants. He stood in the

doorway, blocking escape.

'Got to go, Anthony. Late for school.'

Clara guided Lucia before her like a tiny tug boat. The two of them marched out.

Anthony stood in the hallway, his underpants dangling from his hand like a smeared blue flag of surrender. Without the anger, he felt suddenly dejected. It wasn't the underwear. What did he care, really? It was Clara's indifference. Ever since they'd come back to Clara's native London from New York, at her insistence, Anthony had felt his loneliness becoming a solid thing. Clara and Lucia had each other. Two compact bodies on capable legs, they looked like each other, mimicked each other. Peas in a pod. Like mother, like daughter. Anthony desperately missed his home, its vulgarity and drama, the company of his brothers, the sound turned up to maximum.

He looked down. Bruce was looking up at him, drooling, his tail wagging at the end of his long, misshapen back. Anthony leaned down and drew his fingers down one of the dog's soft, floppy ears, scratched him under the chin, then stood up straight, stuffed the underwear into his dressing gown pocket and headed up to the bedroom to prepare himself for the day.

*

Clara dropped Lucia off at the nursery school, waiting round the corner for the requisite ten minutes to make sure that Lucia, faithful as a small square terrier, didn't escape to try to follow her down the street. Clara was still irritated with Anthony. How come she was somehow laundry captain? Why couldn't he just do his own laundry if he got so upset? It wasn't as if she'd got her two degrees in laundry sorting. Hers had been an academic life before Lucia, a life of grappling with the arcane notions of the mediaeval world. Stupid thing was, she loved her life now. And doing the laundry didn't really bother her. Indeed, folding fresh sheets and underwear, putting it in the airing cupboard, contributing to the daily routine – all of that gave her great satisfaction. She had to catch herself sometimes. Here am I, putting clean sheets in an airing cupboard. Is this really me? Okay, so it wasn't intellectual satisfaction. But it made her happy, nevertheless.

Why was she so cross with Anthony? She felt for him, she really did. Here she was in the country where she had been born and had grown up, ensconced again within a wider family who loved her and welcomed her new family, and there was Anthony, cut off from the supply of humour, chutzpah, energy and soul that New York provided for him. Most importantly, he was cut off from his large family of fellow men, all circulating around his powerfully adoring mother.

Clara's heart suddenly lurched as she thought of Anthony going off into the heart of London, alone, far from home, upset and wearing blue underwear. Clara knew how much this would peck at the corners of his mind all day long. She made a decision to get home quickly before he left for the day, rather than dawdling in a sulk.

When Clara got in, closing the front door behind her as quietly as she could and grabbing Bruce's collar so that his wind was cut off mid-bark, she could hear the shower going full blast. This was her American husband's priority when they moved into the terraced house with the glossy green flock wallpaper. A riot of fleur de lys. The bathroom was a sad little room with a beige bath stained green under the taps.

'Oh man,' Anthony had groaned. 'We gotta get a decent shower put in. How do you guys ever stay clean?'

This was a thing that Clara, with her academic tendency to hedge all things about with alternative possibilities, loved about Anthony. He just said what he thought. No 'on the one hand, on the other hand' dissembling. No disingenuous couching of terms. Out it came. And the job got done. Clara had never been so thoroughly clean in her life.

She hurried into the kitchen to prepare her peace offering,

with the now released Bruce following her in anticipation.

*

Markie's ears were stinging with cold. The snow had started the night before and lay thickly on the ground all through the long next day – a day in which Markie moved from one doorway to the next, from one air vent to the next, trying to stay warm. He had found a spot up by Highbury train station where he'd sat for a while on a cardboard mat, knees scrunched up by his ears, wrapped in the old sleeping bag he'd found down Pentonville Road one time. With his hands pressed to his ears inside the hoodie, he tried to stop the pain. There was no chance of dozing off. There wasn't any food. There wasn't any drink or anything – or anything. He was going to have to get some food.

Do you remember that old lady that gave you chocolates one day – it must have been Christmas – that's it, Christmas and you was on the train, trying to get money, but you said you was hungry, you kept going on about being hungry, doing your noble young man, there but for the grace of god, wouldn't hurt a fly, I'm okay really, just fallen on hard times, act? Well, this old lady, grey hair in a lump on her head, big warm coat, fancy gloves, burrowed about in her bag, then opened a big tin of chocolates, Roses was it, or Quality Street, don't matter, anyway, she shoves this tin under your nose don't she, says 'take a handful, go on.' So you did. Saved them for later. But once you got down the shelter, they got nicked or something, anyway, you only had one left, but it was lovely, green shiny paper and coconut flavour. You remember that.

*

Anthony carried with him the disconsolation of the morning's quarrel as he made his way down One Tree Hill towards Honor Oak Park Station. Why did Clara have to send him off like that? This was not going to be a fun day in any case, working on the accounts of some wingding would-be tax avoider up in Islington. No-one liked paying taxes, godammit,

Anthony mused as he stuck his Oyster card on the reader, but there was such a thing as honour. Or honor, as he would spell it. Honour, like oak, should be a solid thing. So why wasn't Clara being honourable to him?

Standing on the platform, chilly in his lightweight LL Bean jacket, bought for him by Clara in their free-spending New York days, and beloved because of that, Anthony gazed up at the steep embankment, wondering as he always did how on earth he had got from there to here.

*

Markie moved his legs out from under him. They were stiff and sore and Markie grunted as he shoved himself up from the pavement. The snow hadn't settled. There was a slickness to the pavement; flakes were landing on the passing cars, evanescing as they hit the warm metal. Warm people in those cars. Must get warm, shaking his legs, rubbing his hands, walking, striding even to Highbury Station. And hungry. Hungry like the wolf. What? Markie wolf, lean and mean, with limbs that had sinews and skin that stretched over his body like a sausage casing, tight and bursting. But no bread crumbs. No filler. All meat, all meat. Markie meat man. Wolf man Markie. Would die for a burger.

A train is waiting patiently at Platform 1, puffing out its cheeks and breathing out noisily. Get on train. Warmer. No-one on yet, just Markie, stomping up through the open carriages, taking up pole position at the train's head, ready for the long walk down through the carriages, as they bob and clang, duck and dive, ducking and diving, bobbing and clanging. That's Markie, man. Ready now. People crowding on, claiming seats. It's late, they're tired. Time to go home. Lucky home people. Home on train. Home on train. Home on train.

*

Anthony was on his way home. Train packed. It had been a wearing day, unproductive, yet he didn't feel like going home. The morning scene had left a bitter taste in his mouth. It was against the ebullience of his nature to feel this dry and meagre. Oh hell. Look what's coming this way. Young guy. Begging. Get a job man, was Anthony's first thought. His own life hadn't been easy.

The young guy was starting to spout. How he didn't like to beg, but he couldn't get a job. How he was hungry, but had no money. Did anyone have anything to eat?

'I beg your pardon, ladies and gents, but I wouldn't ask if I didn't have to. If you have anything to spare, any change at all, it would be helping me out.'

And he continued down the train, making his speech, bending slightly from the waist, a touch of deference, a touch of pride. Anthony had to admit the kid was good. But as Markie got closer to where Anthony sat, he caught Markie's eye. This was a very, very young man: a boy.

Honor Oak was the next stop. The two people next to Anthony, swaddled in heavy wool and leather against the cold, continued to talk to each other as Markie delivered his lines. You couldn't blame them, but a sudden rancour towards them gripped Anthony, for their comfortable dismissal of the boy.

He put his hand into his jacket pocket to find some cash and his fingers closed around a foil wrapped package. He pulled it out and started to open it. Inside was a large piece of moist, crumbly, dark carrot cake with yellow butter frosting, his all-time favourite. Clara was an ace baker and this was one of her regulars. She made this cake for the purposes of comfort.

Anthony quickly wrapped it up again, looked up into the face of the boy, pressed the cake into his hand.

'It's carrot cake, kid,' he said awkwardly. 'My wife made it.'

Markie took the cake and gave Anthony a tight, nervous grin.

As Anthony watched Markie making his way down the train, he saw him sit down on one of the tip-up seats by the door and start to unwrap the foil.

*

Markie wiped his finger over the frosting that had stuck to the foil and licked it, then sank his teeth into the cake. As he chewed the moist, sweet carrot cake an uneasy sensation sniffed at the side of his brain. Something unfelt in all the years since the separation from his mother. It was the fleeting sensation of safety.

*

It had been hard work, bundling Lucia up into her arctic weather outfit and getting Bruce organized to go for a walk at an unexpected time. This was not the routine and Lucia fought the interruption to bath and bedtime story, while Bruce took some rousing from his post-dinner nap. But Clara was determined. The three of them made their way at different speeds down the snowy street towards the station, Lucia recalcitrant in the squeaky rolls of her winter jacket, trailing and moaning, Bruce pulling ahead, whining excitedly. As they got to Honor Oak Station, hordes of tired people were pushing out of the gate, not looking at anyone, desperate to get by, to get on, to get home. Bruce led the way against the crowd, with Clara and Lucia, her arms held at a forty-five degree angle from her body by the thickness of her jacket, following.

And all of a sudden, there was Anthony, smiling. Clara put Lucia's hand into his, tightened Bruce's lead in her own and the four of them marched out of the station, homeward bound.

FOREST HILL

Mr Forest Hill Station
Peter Morgan

I don't know his name, but that's what the children called him, and I followed suit. We first met him one grey Saturday morning, while I was standing on the platform at Forest Hill Station with my son and daughter, then aged about eleven and nine, waiting for a train to London Bridge for an outing. As we had five minutes to kill, the three of us carried on with a word game we'd started. It was a competition between them and me in which we took turns at naming animals that you might find in a zoo, beginning with each letter of the alphabet. If your opponent couldn't think of an animal you scored a notional point. We weren't really keeping tally, though. It was more a matter of feeling that you were doing well enough. However we were getting near the end of the alphabet and the kids were beginning to feel that they hadn't done well enough compared with Dad and frustration was creeping into their voices.

Glancing round at others waiting on the platform, I encountered the eyes and amused smile of a short, slim man, in his thirties perhaps, who was standing next to us. I suppose he had been following our game for a while. He had sandy hair brushed straight across from a parting, his ears stuck out a bit, and he had large round glasses. He wore a jacket and tie. The general effect was that of someone alert, bookish, and somehow old-fashioned – a 'perpetual student' perhaps.

He widened his smile and directed it at the children who

had now turned to look at him.

'I think you're both doing awfully well at quite a difficult game,' he said. His voice was high-pitched but nicely modulated. They weren't quite sure how to respond to him. Still smiling, and, waggling his eyebrows in a way that made them smile too, he said, 'I wonder – might I join in?'

The children turned to me. 'Well I don't see why not, do you?' I said to them. The man's pleasant intervention had come to all of us as a bit of a relief.

He turned to me, and asked brightly: 'Any special rules I should know about?'

'Well,' I said, 'we allow the names of birds and fishes too. It doesn't strictly have to be something you find in a zoo.' He grinned and nodded.

We progressed through the last few letters, in the course of which the young man displayed marvellous tact in managing to help the children out with their turn, while pretending to have difficulty with his own. When, for instance, I had the first go at the letter 'V' and chose 'vulture', the children's faces fell, but the stranger came to the rescue by prompting them to think of small woodland creatures, which led my daughter to shout 'vole!' in triumph. The man then smacked himself on the forehead with theatrical gusto, exclaiming: 'How stupid of me! I should have kept that for myself!'

The train came in as we finished dealing with the letter 'Y', so we all got into the same compartment. It was my turn to go first again, and once more I saw the children's faces fall, as they realised that there was really only one obvious candidate for 'Z', and that they would finish the game without scoring. I looked at the young man. He grinned and, concealing the gesture from the children, gave me a thumbs-up sign and gestured to me to go ahead. Having developed some confidence in him, I turned to the children.

'Zebra', I said.

'Oh, jolly well done!' said the young man quickly and enthusiastically. 'I mean there's another animal much more commonly found in zoos, so to think of zebra is rather clever!'

We all looked at him in puzzlement. 'What other animal?' my daughter asked. The young man looked at her as if astonished. 'Well, aren't people animals?' he asked in return. My children nodded. 'And aren't there people that you find at every zoo, whose name begins with 'Z'?'

'Zookeepers!' they both shouted as one. Fashioning his expression into one of chagrin, the young man smacked himself on the forehead again. He then pulled some crumpled papers out of his jacket pocket and, telling us that he was due to give a lecture and needed to refresh his memory, he said goodbye and departed for a quieter carriage.

*

I looked out for the young man after that episode, hoping to bump into him again. He'd made a sharp impression on me, and my children too. If one of us made a witty remark, it became a stock response for another to retort 'Well aren't you a regular Mr Forest Hill Station, then!' Over time his name became abbreviated to 'Mr FHS'. My wife would raise her eyebrows and shake her head whenever these exchanges took place.

There were no sightings of Mr FHS for about ten years, however, until I suddenly encountered him at the station again. This must have been around the millennium, I think.

I had just got off a train from Croydon during the evening rush hour and, together with many others, was walking through the ticket hall, when I noticed the young man ahead of me going in the same direction, towards Dartmouth Road. I say 'young' because he still had the almost boyish appearance that I recalled so well, complete with the brushed-across sandy hair, and sticking-out ears. As he skirted the roadway outside the station, however, he was stopped by a middle-aged man, standing with his back to a wall and grasping a bunch of leaflets in one hand. As I came up, the older man, who was dressed in dark clothes, almost as if he were attending a funeral, but not a very smart one, directly addressed the young man in the unnecessarily loud voice that only those of an unconventional religious persuasion can adopt.

'Do you accept that the dead are still with us? That they are all around us?' he intoned. 'Where is there for them to go to, I ask you? They do not go anywhere. They are still here!'

I wondered if the man was heading towards the topic of resurrection. If he was, he didn't get there. The young man stopped, and appeared to take the question seriously. He spoke so fluently that it gave the other man no opportunity to interrupt.

'Look,' he said. 'Since you've been kind enough to give me the benefit of your views on this matter, I shall give you my honest response. Which is, and I do apologise for seeming to contradict you, that my views are almost entirely the opposite. Not completely; but almost. I can, that is to say, happily begin by agreeing wholeheartedly with you when you say that the dead do not go anywhere. Indeed they don't. The problem with your position is that the all-important dimension of time has been left out. The dead don't go anywhere; but the rest of us do. We go on, we carry on, in time, and leave the dead behind. When they died they metaphorically achieved that difficult task of stopping the world and getting off. Now, I'm afraid I must get on. It really has been most kind of you to listen to me.' And he moved off as smoothly as he had spoken.

The older man had hardly moved during the younger's speech. Now he raised his gaze and stared across the vehicles in the station forecourt, adopting a position of dignified silence. I had stopped along with several others, to listen to what the young man had said. As I moved off myself and passed beneath the dignified gaze I felt an unexpected pang of sympathy for its owner.

I rounded the corner into Dartmouth Road, hoping to keep Mr FHS in sight, but he had disappeared, and was nowhere to be seen, even though I glanced into each of the first shops in the road. On getting home I wrote down what he had said and emailed it to the children, who were now both university students, heading it 'Second MFHS Sighting', confident that they would understand the allusion. To my surprise my son wrote a poem about the incident, entitled 'Some Say The Dead Are All Around', and encapsulating Mr FHS's argument. It was printed in a student magazine.

*

I continued to keep a look-out for Mr FHS, but I had all but forgotten him when, after a gap of almost eleven years this time, I spotted him. I was leaving Forest Hill Station once more, although on this occasion it was lunchtime. It was raining, not heavily but quite persistently, and on a whim I decided that instead of going home, where nobody else would be in, I would stroll round the corner from the station to the Caribbean food stall in Dartmouth Road. I'd never tried it before. When I got there I found it had a canopy to keep the rain off, and no other customers. On enquiring from the cheerful woman behind the counter whether I could simply stand and eat something there on the pavement, the answer was encouragingly affirmative. I browsed the unfamiliar menu – calypso fried chicken, jerk wings, meat or vegetable patty, or curry goat. I chose vegetable patty.

While I waited three noisy young West Indian men arrived who joked and joshed with the woman behind the counter as they ordered their food. The rain had eased a bit.

Shortly afterwards, a middle-aged white couple halted at the stall too. The man had dark, intense eyes, a straggly beard, and unkempt black hair streaked with white. He was wearing a trench coat buttoned up to the neck; the coat had seen better days. His wife (as I took her to be) was more conventional looking, wearing a tent-like black coat over a long blue shabby skirt. They looked at the menu and seemed to confer silently over what they would have. Speaking very clearly, the wife informed the woman behind the counter that her husband would have some curry goat. She didn't order anything for herself.

The man's food came after a while in one of those plastic containers that fast food places use. There was no lid as, like me, he was going to eat it there and then. Instead of using the fork he was given, however, he raised the container, tilted it, and began to eat directly from it. The young men stopped talking among themselves and stared at him. The woman behind the counter and I glanced quickly at each other and then both looked away. One of the young men laughed loudly and the eating man turned sharply towards him. His beard was already well smeared with food and the increased tilt of the container and sudden turn sent some of his sauce splattering onto the pavement near the rest of us, sending a small splash to mark a snazzy pair of shoes in the process. (They weren't mine, of course.)

'Hey!' said the wearer of the snazzy footwear.

The eating man carried on as if he had not heard. I tensed myself for a scene. But there, suddenly, was Mr Forest Hill Station. I had the impression that he could only just have arrived, walking down Dartmouth Road towards the station, and coming up behind me. I was quite startled: he was instantly recognisable, even after all this time. He seemed to take the situation in very quickly, and he moved towards the eating man and began to speak to him in the same fluent way that I had witnessed before.

'Look, I am terribly sorry to interrupt your meal, but I do have to ask you what you are up to. Can you enlighten me, perhaps?' He allowed a brief pause, in which the eating man made no attempt to answer. Then he carried on.

'Basically, you know, human beings are divided between their human and animal aspects. One of the most important things we have to do in our lives is to arrive at a proper balance between the two. You appear to have chosen to adopt a heavily animal-oriented disposition. It is not possible for you to achieve such a state however, for even if you think you are an animal, it follows that you are not one: animals *cannot* think about their state of being.' And once again he moved smoothly off.

The eating man stopped chewing, the container still raised to his mouth. His wife gently removed the plastic container from him and placed it on the counter. He didn't resist when she took his arm and led him away.

I immediately went home and emailed the children. My daughter, who was now taking a part-time course in philosophy, used the anecdote in an essay. Not only did it raise a bit of a laugh when she read the essay out in a weekend seminar, but it led to an animated debate about the differences between human beings and animals.

We all read the essay, and had a lively family discussion the next time we were all together. My daughter adopted an annoying tone of superiority in this discussion, until I observed that Mr FHS would not have spoken like that.

*

I had a dream last night in which Mr Forest Hill Station stopped me on the bridge over the platforms. Dusk was falling and we were alone.

'Human beings, you know,' he said, 'are caught between desire and claims to grace; and by the struggle to articulate their claims, in loaded language and a loaded world. Each world language is a Tower of Babel all its own. I claim no special freedom from these snares. I do my best when I see people struggle with words that will not help a soul; or struggle for those that will.' He paused.

'I like it here. Forest Hill, One Tree Hill, Honor Oak. There used to be a forest here stretching down to Croydon: the Great North Wood. One needs to see a forest entire. And yet understand each tree in its smallest detail. Every branch, each thorn.

'You see, the word *forest* doesn't mean trees, it means *outdoors, beyond – unfenced-in.*' Unsatisfied, he sought another

143

word. 'The wild.'

He paused again.

'Forests remind us, I think, that we are the animal that, as we strive to conquer the wild, choose to forget the wildness at our own core.'

With that he faded, *on the blowing of a horn*, which, as I woke, merged with the sound of his voice, still echoing – seemingly from the Great North Wood itself.

SYDENHAM

Actress
Andrew Blackman

Agnes was late again. She sat peering through misted windows at the rain-smeared back gardens beyond. The train was only a few hundred yards from her stop, but hadn't moved for ten minutes now. Still, Agnes felt glad to be inside, away from all the bustle of the South London streets. She couldn't take that any more, not since that day when some idiot chatting on his mobile phone had crashed into her and sent her flying into the gutter with all her shopping. He'd stopped and apologized in that obsequious way that young people do these days: 'I'm reeeaaaallly sorry, I'm reeeaaaallly sorry.' But he'd kept the phone dangling close to his ear all the time, just moving the mouthpiece slightly to the side out of consideration for his friend. And of course he hadn't helped her pick up all the tins and bags that were scattered all over the road. Since then, Agnes was always wary. Instead of walking, she took the train a single stop from Forest Hill to Sydenham, and then took a minicab the rest of the way.

Of course, once she'd been one of those inconsiderate young people herself, dashing along, late for some opening-night party or gala dinner, sometimes late even for the play she was acting in. 'That's Agnes,' they'd say when she arrived. 'Always late.' She smiled to herself. She'd been good-looking in those days. She always noticed how men turned to stare as she ran by, her long, brown hair streaming out behind her and her skirt billowing out just enough to give a glimpse of her long, thin legs. Yes, she cut quite a figure in those days. And she knew it. Whenever anyone joked about the men swarming around her like flies, her stock response was, 'Yes, and I love to swat 'em.' Never failed to get a laugh.

She'd swatted quite a few in her time, some of them pretty badly. Poor Charlie Barker. He'd got the worst of it. Most of them got swatted once, twice at the most, and then stayed away, but not Charlie. He must have been besotted with her, poor thing. He kept coming back and coming back, and each time she swatted him away more disdainfully. He claimed he'd met her in some pub or something, not that she could remember. There had been so many men in so many pubs. And besides, Charlie wasn't exactly that memorable. He had wild blond hair, jutting out in all directions like a mad professor. His face was pale and gaunt, making his large blue eyes stand out all the more as he stared at her from behind thick-rimmed glasses. He always wore the same brown sleeveless pullover on top of some crumpled shirt and stained corduroy trousers. He didn't exactly have a stammer, but it seemed that way because he spoke in such slow, halting sentences, choosing each word as if his life depended on getting precisely the right one.

In short, hardly her type. How would he look on her arm as they went to the premiere of her latest film? What would he be able to say to Orson Welles or Clark Gable? As she always used to say to him, 'Where I'm going, you won't be able to follow me.' He'd always reply with some romantic nonsense about following her anywhere, and claiming that they weren't really so different – as if he really knew her anyway! They'd barely exchanged any words, and all of those had been hostile, on her part at least.

But whatever she said, he just kept on coming back. It got so bad that her friend Linda even took pity on him and asked him out herself. That was unheard-of in those days, for a woman to give up her dignity like that. Even worse, he turned her down. Said he would be lying to her and to himself if he took her out, because he'd be thinking of Aggie the whole time. After that, her friends practically pleaded with her to give the poor fellow a chance, but she wouldn't budge. She'd been swatting men away since she was a child, and she didn't know any other way. It was who she was.

Then everything changed. It was her twenty-eighth birthday and her friends had taken her out to celebrate both her birthday and a new part she'd got, playing a jilted lover in some West End musical. It looked like the break she'd been waiting for. She felt invincible that night, in her flowing midnight-blue dress and with her hair elegantly tied up to expose her soft white neck. 'You really are the belle of the ball tonight,' one old man had said to her as she came off the dance floor after one number. But it was the young men she cared about. As she danced with one, she was always trying to spot the next one out of the corner of her eye. She wanted to see who was looking at her, who desired her, who would ask her to dance next.

She hadn't noticed Charlie, though. He just appeared in front of her suddenly as the music from the last song died. He was wearing a creased black tie and what looked like an Edwardian smoking jacket. His blond hair was shining and plastered flat to his head. He'd used so much Brylcreem to tame those unruly curls that she could even see where some excess had dripped onto his shoulder. His trousers were pressed for once, and his shoes sparkled. Even so, she thought he was lucky they'd let him in with that jacket. He cleared his throat, looked at his shoes for a second, and then opened up the box and held it out towards her. The diamond was so small that for a moment she wasn't even sure that it was an engagement ring, but then she saw it protruding almost apologetically from its base.

'I love you, Agnes,' he said. 'I've always loved you. I know you keep telling me no, but I can't help it. I want to spend my life with you, and I think if you give me a chance you'll find I'm not as bad as you think. Maybe you'll even love me one day like

I love you. I don't want you to decide now, but please at least take the ring, and consider my offer.'

She just looked straight back at him and said calmly and deliberately, 'Charles Barker, I will not marry you. Nor will I consider marrying you.' And as she turned away from him, back straight, head in the air, she'd felt like a queen. Graceful, elegant, untouchable. There were a few stifled chuckles as Charlie backed away, but mostly an awestruck silence. In those few seconds before the band struck up again, she'd felt all the eyes in the room fixed on her, as if she were the sun and the whole restaurant was revolving around her, drawn to her beauty and yet afraid of her power.

They found Charlie face-down in the mud flats of the Thames estuary the next morning. A couple of fishermen had spotted him through the early-morning mists, washed up on the shore with all the rotting wood, dead cats and other detritus that had been flushed out of the city that night. 'Accidental death,' they said. Apparently poor Charlie had so much whisky in him that he wouldn't have known what happened to him. Some wag at the funeral even joked they'd better not light any matches or the whole place would go up. But Agnes knew it was no accident.

After Charlie died, she kept waiting for her life to fall apart. She thought her friends would desert her, she'd lose her job, the men would stop looking at her, and she'd find herself old and lonely and penniless. She thought she'd be punished, or at least forced to admit that she'd killed another human being, more or less. But it didn't happen like that. Her acting career, such as it was, trundled along as if Charlie had never existed. The few people who even knew about his death said it added to her allure. Her friends mostly rushed to her defence too: 'How could you possibly have known what he was going to do? You'd swatted him so many times before and he'd never reacted like that. You mustn't blame yourself. You mustn't think about it anymore. You should get on with your life.' And so on and so forth. Only her friend Linda seemed to blame her, although she never said anything directly. Linda married and moved up north, and that was the last Agnes ever heard about her.

As for the men, they kept swarming, just like before. And she kept swatting, just like before. The only difference was in the way she felt. She didn't feel like a queen any more, and suspected she never would, no matter how much she kept acting like one. She didn't get satisfaction from all the attention any more, or even from the swatting. For the first time, she just wished all the men would leave her alone. About a year after Charlie's death, she finally realized that the axe never would fall. It would just grind, very slowly.

Agnes came to with a jolt as the train lurched forward, then came to a halt at the next signal. The illusion of progress. It was hot on the train now, a pungent kind of heat, rich with the aromas of evaporating rain and diesel fumes. She would be very late indeed.

These days, though, people didn't smile indulgently and say 'That's Agnes – always late.' She didn't have parties to go to any more, or dinners, or soirees. She had doctor's appointments, hairdressing appointments, meetings with social workers. Those people rolled their eyes, irritated at having to be burdened by some batty old woman and her problems, and even more irritated at being kept waiting. Some lingering notion of respect for the elderly usually kept them from saying anything too rude, but the restrained, tongue-biting courtesy was almost worse. When she was young and beautiful, she could get away with murder. Now, she sometimes felt she had to apologise for still being alive.

It was a long time now since her looks had gone. The soft red glow of her cheeks had hardened into dull grey putty. Great crevasses crisscrossed her forehead. Her skin sagged. Her beautiful, enchanting curves had become misshapen lumps. If she wore a billowing dress these days, men would only gaze in disgust at her varicose veins. She was old. Very old. The flirtatious glances had stopped so long ago that she couldn't even remember the last one. Funny how there must have been a last time, and she would never even have known it. One last, lustful look from some unknown man. It should have been a momentous event, the end of her youth, the end of her beauty. But it passed unnoticed, one of a thousand glances. By the time she realized there would never be another one, it was gone from her memory.

In just the same way, she didn't know when she realised she would never be a film star. Was it when she hit thirty? Forty? Fifty? Was it when she had to call her agent instead of him calling her? Was it when she had to switch agents? When she was first cast as the lead actress's mother? When she started teaching drama at the local secondary modern? Maybe it was all of these and none of them. At each point she'd always felt that it was just a temporary detour on her way to the top. She had to. She couldn't just go through life and not do anything, not be noticed, not affect anything except Charlie Barker. That couldn't be it. With all her talent, her looks, her energy, with all the things she had to say and do, she couldn't just fail. But somewhere along the way, she had. As it turned out, the musical role that she'd found out about just before her twenty-eighth birthday was as close as she got. She could still remember the applause the first night, the flowers thrown on stage, the whistles and shouts, the backstage clamour. She even got some good reviews.

If a film producer had stopped by on one of those nights, before the show went stale, before she lost the part to some younger actress, then maybe things would have been different. But he didn't, and so she wasn't Agnes Hillier: movie star. She was Agnes Hillier: case number 28763921009. Or Agnes Hillier: *probably got another couple of years at most with that heart of hers*. Or Agnes Hillier: *you know, that dotty old lady who comes in to*

get her hair done up like a princess every week, is always late, and
gawd knows why she bothers to do it like that at her age anyway.

She still didn't know how it came to this. She didn't mess it up herself. She'd been making small steps in the right direction, but then time had come along and swept it all away. If she'd only had more time, she could've made it. She was sure of that. Instead it had just slipped away. Like Charlie, dragged out to sea, pulled under by the current even if he did try to kick against it, probably not even knowing which breath was his last. Like Charlie, only in slow motion. She laughed: a dry, bitter laugh. She'd never thought of it that way before.

And now, as she sat on the train in the middle of a world that she barely even recognized and Charlie definitely wouldn't, she wondered what would have been so bad about giving him a chance. Just letting him take her out a few times, to see what happened. Maybe it would have been nice to give up the acting for a while, to stop swatting men away as people had come to expect. Maybe her life would have been different. Most likely it would have been disastrous, but maybe he'd even be sitting next to her today, holding her bags, teasing her about always being late.

CRYSTAL PALACE

She Didn't Believe in Ghosts
Jacqueline Downs

Like any place nearby and far away, long ago and right now, Crystal Palace is full of ghosts. Not the ghosts of people – Ann Buckingham didn't believe in ghosts, even though she felt like one herself at times, as she receded into a life that had turned out to be as translucent as baby skin; as pale as a corpse: undeveloped.

So, she didn't believe in the white sheet with the eyeholes cut out, or finding belongings in the sitting room rearranged, or the glass being pushed around a Ouija board, or 'help me' lipsticked on the bathroom mirror. As far as Ann Buckingham was concerned, when you were dead you were dead; there was no coming back. For Ann, the ghosts of Crystal Palace were in the just-visible roots of the Palace itself, and in the White Hart hotel, in the site of the old windmill, in the homely cottages that once lined Westow Hill; all replaced by the beauty parlours and cafés and estate agents that framed her life.

Missing people were different; missing people were neither dead nor alive; they inhabited that uncanny plane between what is known and what is unknown. They lived in the minds of the people who missed them and they became living ghosts, neither fully present nor fully absent.

Mostly, Ann felt like the missing. Where once she'd been a fully-drawn person, life and its disappointments and losses had reduced her to an outline. She did the same thing over and over every day, drifting through her routine like a white feather on a breeze. The breakfast made, the washing up done, the laundry on. She was living a life that had been written by someone from an earlier time.

At a loss for what to do as her world narrowed, she rode the Overground from its first stop in Crystal Palace all the way to Highbury & Islington, and back. The orange poles and seemingly never-ending tunnel of seats, uninterrupted by carriage doors, stretched before her eyes, and she felt as though she was being recalled to somewhere she faintly knew.

Ann studied the other passengers, their faces animated in conversation, their voices floating, dislocated; mouths moving, words not matching. She looked at two teenage girls linked together by a white wire extending to one ear each, nodding in time, their lips forming an indecipherable language. Nothing worked as it should; nothing seemed like anything she fully recognised.

Finding nothing but the end of the line, she abandoned the trains and took to sitting in the local library when she should have been ironing, or shopping for fresh fish, or making the beds, or – in a different life – visiting a Parisian hotel with a lover.

She had started by browsing the books, picking them off the shelves, dipping into the worlds they offered her; worlds whose hazy edges seemed familiar. Then she discovered the postcard images from long ago of this place that she knew right now. The carriage-like cars with their oversized wheels frozen on the uneven road by the streets she walked daily; the blurred figures in long dark coats and stiff hats; the cottages and cobbles and churches.

These postcards of the days when one century had become another, which in turn had already passed, led her elsewhere: to the archives of newspapers and the microfiche with its luminous glare giving off the ghosts of stories past. It took her a while to accustom her wrist to the machine, and for some time the pages spun before her at dizzying speed. Her gaze flickered over the screen as she tried to make some sense of the words on it, until her wrist, and her eyes, came to light on a page from the *Norwood Review* from the 27th of May 1900. Her attention was caught by a headline.

'FOURTH LOCAL MAN STILL MISSING'
and in smaller print
'mystery deepens, police no closer to solution'.

The article outlined the case: the four men had been part of the Upper Norwood Literary and Scientific Society which met in Foresters Hall on Westow Street, under the presidency of Arthur Conan Doyle. When the writer had resigned in 1894, this group of men had retained their links to the hall with a variety of clubs and organisations, trying to settle on something of interest. When one of the men, Alfred Cooper, had visited Paris at the end of 1895, he had seen on a makeshift screen the first flickering movements of babies eating breakfast, of leaves fluttering in the breeze, of workers leaving a factory, and he brought back with him to Crystal Palace a desire to share these wonderful dreams with his friends.

'We sat in the dark together, as one, and we watched as these photographs moved and danced before us, and it was as though ghosts were coming to life before my eyes,' he is reported to have said at the inaugural meeting of the Crystal Ciné Club.

Ann read on, her wrist taking her back and forth between the unfolding of the mystery. The men had met regularly, spending the end of the century buying the equipment necessary to watch these one-reelers with their primitive narratives, a combination of realism and fantasy. Then, between February and May, they had disappeared from public life. One by one they no longer attended their jobs or their club; they no longer took in the clear air in the park or the blackened smoke of Church Road. As each one left, the others continued, making no comment, appearing resigned to the circumstances, until they, too, took their leave. Their families reported no sightings of them. Cooper and his friends, Samuel Graham, Thomas

Bateson and William Adams, had simply vanished. Ann scoured the photographs that accompanied the stories, noting the tidy beard and trimmed moustache of Cooper, Adams's Homburg, Bateson and Graham's greatcoats.

She tucked her long, red hair behind her ears, scribbled the details in her notebook, sketched the men in the charcoal of her pencil, capturing their likenesses, printing their names beneath each face, frozen on the lined page.

It was only closing time that drove her back home. There, she did what she had to do, but it was as though someone else's hands made the dinner; someone else's eyes watched the small screen in the living room; someone else's voice held conversations with itself. When she slept that night she dreamt of trains arriving at stations, of babies being fed, of bearded men in tall hats, and then blankness, nothingness.

The next morning, she made tea, as she always did. She glanced up at the window, where the steam from the kettle was clouding her view. When she looked again, she saw the merest trace of letters, what appeared to her startled eyes as *C, I, N*, before they weakened and disappeared, trickling down the pane, like tears.

She was at the library doors when they opened, back on the microfiche, back with the *Norwood Review*. After the end of May 1900 the story seemed also to disappear from view. The police had given up and so had the reporters. There was nothing left to see.

She made her way down Westow Hill to Anerley Hill, passing the museum, where the ornate roof of the rail station caught her eye as always, encouraging her to take another journey into the light. Although the ground was smooth and the path clear, she tripped, falling sideways into the gate at the museum's entrance.

'If I was a character in a film,' she thought, 'I would have to take this as a sign.'

So, like a character in a film, she took the fall as a sign and she went through the gate, over the pebbles, round the back and up the stairs into the rooms of glass cabinets, and carefully printed explanations, and models of the Crystal Palace. There was nothing she could see about the Literary and Scientific Society or the Crystal Ciné Club.

She spoke to the man behind the counter, the only person in the museum, about her discovery in the library, and he took her to a door off the side of the main room. Unlocking it, and gesturing to the winding staircase behind it, he said:

'Up there you'll find a storeroom. There are some old trunks, from way back. Have a look around, you never know what you'll find.' And before she could take her first step towards the staircase he was gone.

She was there for hours, rooting through boxes and cases and trunks, finding nothing of consequence. Sitting on the floor, leaning against one of the bigger trunks, she felt something give at the small of her back, and turning, she saw that a panel in the side of the trunk had shifted slightly. She pushed it gently and it gave a little further. She pushed again and it moved entirely, yielding up a gap large enough to get her hand in. She felt her way into the space, and when she pulled her hand out she was surprised to find in her fingers a tiny reel of film. Without thinking, she placed it in her purple satchel, made her way down the staircase, out of the door and into the main room. There was a woman at the counter this time and she was clearly taken aback.

'How did you get up there? That's supposed to be locked,' she said. Ann smiled as warmly as she was able to in this newly chilly atmosphere.

'I had an arrangement,' she said, 'with the manager.' And she passed through the room and out of the main door before the woman could protest that she was the manager and there had been no such arrangement and…

Outside, Ann breathlessly made her way down the hill and into the park. As she approached the roots of the Palace she saw the man from the museum moving towards her, his features seeming slightly out of focus to her tired eyes. As he drew level with her, a piece of card fell from his hand. She stopped to pick it up, and as she reached out to return it she saw that he had already gone. On the card she read the words that took her to the next stop.

A week of washing and cooking and ironing later and Ann was in a night-black room in a near-deserted building off Church Road, weaving the thread of the film around the reels on an ancient editing table. As she clicked the machine into life the film appeared at once. It was grainy and jumpy, the novelty of its movements enhanced and exaggerated by the damage done by the passing of time. She moved closer to the screen as the footage of the magnificent front of the Palace sharpened into view.

At first there was just the Palace and the grass and the wide, open space of the park. Birds made their stuttering flight across the sky; trees stretched and bent, their branches shuddering in the wind.

Then her eyes were caught by what appeared to be human shapes. The figures moved slowly, as though weighed down by more than just a century of mystery. Two figures wore greatcoats, the tails flapping in the breeze, another had on a Homburg. The last had his face turned away from the camera. She rewound the film and the figures reversed and disappeared before making their appearance again. And again, and again.

They repeated these actions, moving back and forth, back and forth, although Ann was no longer touching the machine. She remembered the greatcoats and the Homburg from the newspaper reports.

As the missing men walked their interminable walk

beyond the Palace, across the grounds and back, again and again, the last one turned, and looked directly into the camera. He had a tidy beard and a trimmed moustache. His mouth opened and she saw the words form, as faintly but distinctly as the letters on the window pane in her kitchen. 'Help us.' She jumped back, her stomach dropping like a bird shot from its nest.

'Help us.'

Before she could stop the reel turning she noticed a fifth figure, a woman, not mentioned in the reports.

The woman's clothes were different, more modern, and in colour.

As the female figure approached the camera, unacknowledged by the men, Ann was able to see her more clearly than she had ever seen anything in her life: the blue skirt, the black shoes, the purple satchel. As she saw the red hair of the woman frozen against the backdrop of the Palace, she knew. She was lost forever.

PENGE WEST

Penge Tigers
Adrian Gantlope

There were two of them now and he knew it would not be long before they were joined by more. He couldn't exactly see them, but they were definitely there, their eyes fixed on him from the darkest corner of the room. They paced silently and hid cunningly. Except, six times an hour when the train rattled by, they talked to each other quietly, as if expecting their sounds to be masked. But, despite the train noise, he heard their terrible low growls. He understood them clearly enough. They were growing impatient and were hungry.

They were waiting for him to give up.

They didn't want to wait much longer.

He wished he could go outside again. To go out into the extra-ordinary ordinariness of the damp spring night. He wished he could walk down the stairs, open the front door and step out into the street, and take in un-funked air.

He would walk to the park.

No, he would run, breathing in great lungfuls of cold damp London air.

He would run with his children, after all it was what they always had done. The boys had bloomed here, like the flowers and trees in the park. They had been pushed in their buggies, then toddled then walked then scootered then cycled then ran over every section of the park. He would ask his boys to hold his hands. He would hold two of them tight, Joseph to his left, little

Paul to his right. He would ask the eldest, Miles, to take Paul's other hand, and take the outside.

A glowing responsibility for his little big man.

They would run in a human paperchain into the park and up the steep hill to the children's zoo. They would stop at the top and hold their hips and lean forwards until they got their breath back. Joseph, the liveliest, would pause just for a moment before running around again. Pulling faces and pulling the shirts of the other two until they hit him or collapsed in laughter, usually both.

Once, when just a tiny tot, Paul kissed a petting sheep in the zoo. He planted his lips directly on its blackened teeth. Every time they went afterwards, Miles and Joseph would tease Paul, daring him to snog the sheep again. The zoo kept dwarf goats, and Joseph would rush at them, daring them to butt him. Once one did, and the bruises took weeks to go, and the memory never went at all. Joseph didn't much like the zoo after that. And later the zoo had llamas, which were interesting to look at, but anxious and flighty and spat.

He and the boys decided they didn't like llamas.

Or any live animals, really.

And they hadn't visited in a while.

Quite a while.

There was now a third tiger. It had entered the room as quietly as it could manage while the last train had gone past. Even though it thought it was hidden, he could smell it as it crept past his bed, its breath rank and ketotic.

After the zoo he and the boys would run down and along the lake, past the dinosaurs and all the other prehistoric creatures cast of concrete which loomed on the miniature islands. The monsters. One night, a bit like this one, they had sneaked over the fence and had a midnight feast among the iguanodons. They had eaten monster food. Boiled egg eyeballs, spaghetti guts in blood sauce, Monster Munch and jelly brains.

He had prepared it, and packed it into a scary satchel.

They loved the monsters, much more than the real animals in the zoo. His boys had learned the name of every one of the creatures, those that had been built, those which had been removed decades before after falling into disrepair, and those that should have been there: Benjamin Waterhouse Hawkins' uncomissioned creations hadrosauri, glyptodons, mammoths, and the terrifying smilodon.

Back home, the boys would draw monsters while he prepared their meal. Although Miles was the better artist, he would always take care to be fair, praising every picture evenly. He had kept all the pictures. His favourite was a joint effort named 'Smilodon slays Mammoth'. The sabre-toothed cat, drawn by Miles had formidable and impossibly long teeth and was ready to spring. Joseph's mammoth, wide-eyed, could only wait for the inevitable end.

'Tiger-dinner, daddy!' Paul had said, pointing at the mammoth. Paul was very proud of the grass that he had drawn for the smilodon to stand on.

Another tiger had come in. It lay at the side of his bed, out of sight. He could hear it breathing, ragged and shallow.

His boys couldn't be in the house anymore. Maria must have taken them. Although he wanted them here, at least they were safe wherever they were. He had almost lost track of exactly when he had last seen her. It must have been seven nights ago.

Whenever it was, she had cried, and he had cried.

And two nights ago, the first tiger had come.

It was Maria who had chosen their property. A solid and dependable property, paid for by his solid and dependable accountancy practice, which he could run in a solid and dependable way from the property. His study looked over the lavender bushes and red hot pokers and the many other plants and shrubs which were chosen and planted by her and were a joy to the eye. The property was yellow London brick, three stories, set off from the road and apart from other houses. Not far from the good school where, she had decided, their little boys would one day go. She decided what to remodel in their property, and when. She arranged and hosted their dinner parties, where their friends, or perhaps acquaintances, admired the kitchen, and the decoration of the hall, and the setting of the garden, and the property itself.

An oasis in South-East London, they would say.

And they would admire Maria who was a beautiful and gracious host.

He could hear another one, scratching against the door. The other tigers rose, restless, and growled quietly when the train went past.

She, who had chosen him, and had chosen the property, had also chosen someone else. He never knew a name, or whether the someone else was he or a succession of hes. They never talked directly about that. It was unspoken that he would not mention the nights she came in late, hours after he had fed the boys, bathed them, then tucked them into their beds. He would not ask about the weekends she went to stay with a special friend. It was his role to do what he did well. To be solid and dependable, to work and take care of the bills, and to love the boys. In truth he could bear these arrangements. She needed to do what she needed to do, and he was grateful that she did it privately and that when she had done what she needed to do, she always came back.

To him who needed her.

And to the boys, who needed her.

And while she was gone he had the boys, and the park and the property, and his solid and dependable work.

And when she was back, with him she was affectionate and attentive, particularly when they had guests.

But one day she decided to leave.

She told him he was too dull, as if he didn't already know that. She told him that she had found someone else, as if he didn't already know that.

And that the someone else was kinder than him.

Which surprised him.

She blamed him for turning her into a mare, only fit to have one child after another, and he had made her become a drudge and that she couldn't take it anymore.

Which surprised him.

And that because she had enough of him and the boys, she thought that she needed to go away for a while because she didn't know anymore who she was, or even what she was capable of, and didn't trust herself not do something really really stupid.

So he let her go. As if there was ever an option.

And now he feared the tigers, waiting for him to give up. He couldn't move. Almost as bad as the fear was his thirst. Even if he had dared cry out, he wasn't sure that his dry throat could produce much sound.

She had come back to get some things and he sat on the bed and watched her take some of her clothes from the wardrobe, and pack her cosmetics and her favourite jewellery, the amber. He had bought it for her, spending hours sourcing it from the internet, mostly directly from amber houses in the East. She always wore the largest pendant, a huge rounded piece containing a mosquito, at the most important dinner parties in their property.

As she packed it, he was glad that she still liked what he had given her.

He thought for a moment that it must mean she wasn't really leaving him.

Miles, Joseph and Paul were in the bedroom also, happy to see their mum again. They watched her too, excited about her new adventure, without understanding it properly. She sent them downstairs to play.

She told him she had made some new decisions. It was simple, she said. She wanted the boys with her, she wanted to move back in and she wanted him to move out.

And he would pay the bills.

She said that he should get out of the property and told him that it would be good for him. He might think about taking a holiday, go out more, stretch his wings. Maybe find someone new himself. Someone nice.

Which surprised him, Maria was nice.

Another tiger had come in. Now the room was packed with them, he could hear them rubbing against each other as they paced around the bed. Rough fur scraped against rough fur like the sound of a broom on carpet.

They had argued. She cried. He cried.

No he had said.

And he told her she was a whore and someone who was not fit to look after children.

And that he would not give her a single penny, or even let her see the boys again.

And he told her to go.

Which she did.

More tigers. So many that they were practically on the bed. They no longer waited for the trains to go by to roar. Their growling filled the room. Their smell was unbearable, and the heat from their bodies seared.

And he called out, but his voice made little noise because his throat was so dry.

And no-one could hear him, apart from the tigers.

ANERLEY

Birdland
Joan Taylor-Rowan

He said it right to her face, 'I'm sorry Sal but it's over.'

She looked up at him, stung. It was barely three weeks since Valentine's Day, his card was still sitting on the mantelpiece. Ralph was putting on his coat, his face turned away from hers,

'I mean just look around you – you've turned into bloody Ms Marple'. She grabbed his arms, tears prickling her eyes, and pressed her face into his coat. It smelled like kicked-up leaves.

'I'll try harder, Ralph,' she said, 'I'll try and be –' her voice trailed off. What did he want her to be? She tried to imagine herself in stockings, her hair straightened. He pushed her gently away and cuffed her cheek.

'Don't try and be anything.'

She wiped her face, 'Yeah, I'll just look for men as boring as me shall I?'

He winced. 'I'm sorry Sal, I really am.'

And the next thing she remembered was sound: the door closing, the thump of his feet on the stairs, his swearing as he rescued the overburdened coat stand, the letterbox clatter, the silence. She stood in the centre of the room wondering how the morning had suddenly turned out like that. He'd been about to go out and buy croissants for them and then suddenly it was over. She tried to remember the sequence of events. She'd filled the kettle and while waiting for it to boil (an infinite amount of time – because she'd forgotten to turn it on) she'd started reading the book on garden birds that she'd bought on the way home yesterday. Eventually he'd come out grumpy and sour-breathed and found her there. He'd switched on the kettle and stomped off to the toilet but hadn't said a word. She'd made the coffee and taken it in. They'd lain listening to Radio 4, the morning show that made her laugh sometimes. She'd sensed something, she realised that now, but had chosen not to acknowledge it – a withdrawing of attention, the kind of coolness that normally preceded a criticism. And then he rolled out of bed, showered and was dressed in minutes. He must have said something about buying croissants, which is why she'd rummaged for change and jumped out of bed to give it to him, and then he'd dropped the bombshell and her coins had fallen onto the floor. She should have bought the croissants yesterday – but surely you couldn't break up over croissants.

A bird sang suddenly and she ran to the window grabbing the binoculars that stood on the ledge. She rubbed the lenses with her pyjama top so she could see more clearly. It was a greenfinch on the branch overhanging the fence. It was the spring call, just exactly like it sounded on the free CD of garden birds she'd got from the Guardian. He's after a mate, she thought. She closed her eyes. Ralph. She wondered if the greenfinch ever got it wrong. She thought of Ralph's smooth skin, his hands holding her fingers in the early days. She took off the binoculars. Christ, she was twenty-five and watching garden birds in her pyjamas – blue brushed cotton covered in blackbirds. She'd go down to the shops on Anerley Road, get a haircut, buy a lipstick.

The room was a mess, clothes in heaps, toppled cities of books. She grabbed sweatpants, a puffa jacket, trainers. In the bathroom her red eyes and pale skin accused her. 'Jesus Sally – look at the state of you,' she said to her reflection, as she tied her greasy hair back and added shampoo to her mental list.

Outside the air was crisp and the gleaming green shoots were just beginning to extend themselves past last year's growth

– she could almost hear the sap, and the bare branches vibrating with the life inside. She shoved her hands into her pockets. She'd make an effort: play the game of birds and bees. She scrubbed up well – wasn't that how she snared him in the first place? He didn't know her shoes were borrowed and crippling, and the wired bra like a birdcage.

She walked down the road past number 24 and checked the hole in the dead trunk for signs of activity – fresh droppings – that meant nesting. At number 28 she paused again peering in between the boughs to check out the bird table. It was empty but then something else caught her attention. Closer to her in the leaf litter under the beech tree there was rustling in the leaves. Her heart began to beat – could it be a hedgehog?

She'd last seen a live hedgehog when she was seven years old. It was snuffling its nose into a bowl of cat-food outside the back door of her 1960s semi while the cat arched its back in horror. It had seemed magical to her that this little beast had sauntered onto their estate, trailing its scents of the hedgerows into her suburban garden. Ralph had stared at her when she told this story. A party – his workmates – late at night a bit drunk – best and worst moments. His expression had been a mixture of mortification and contempt, his cheeks had pinked,

'Gypsies had the right idea,' his friend George said, 'baked them like potatoes.' Ralph had snorted into his beer.

'Oh that's mean', Gina crooned, 'don't listen to him Sally, I think hedgehogs are cute.' She leaned forward, her brown breasts loose inside her silk shift dress. Ralph drank them in and returned her glance. Sally gulped down her red wine until the room spun.

The leaves moved again, but it was hard to see. She doubled over, her shoulders level with the break in the hedge and tried to lean into the gap. The garden was overgrown and the house, a big white one with columns reared up out of it. Down the side entrance she could see more garden and possibly a pond. The leaves jumped again. She strained forward trying to get a better look.

'And may I ask what you think you're doing?'

She turned around; a policeman stood next to his bicycle watching her. She suddenly saw herself through his eyes, a girl in dirty street clothes, hair in a Croydon face-lift – as Ralph once called it – speccing out some upmarket flats. His face had that same pained look as Ralph's.

'I love nature,' she blurted out.

His face creased a little more, the words tiny blows to his composure.

'I, I thought I saw a hedgehog under the bushes,' she added, flinging her hand out behind her – 'there were rustlings.'

He raised his eyebrows, 'rustlings were there?'

She turned to the gap in the hedge and beckoned him over. He sighed, looked up the street and then leaned his bicycle against the wall. He peered in to the garden. His jacket smelled slightly of aftershave.

'See there,' she said excitedly, just as the leaves flew, and scattered. Two birds, one mounted on the other skittered out in front of them.

'Oh,' she said pulling back suddenly, 'it was just birds, uh…mating.'

He sighed and brushed himself down.

'It's spring,' she said, blushing, 'it's the natural order of things.'

'Trust me to get Bill Oddie,' he said.

'I don't always dress like this,' she said, aware that he hadn't compared her to Kate Humble.

'Like what?' he said.

She noticed him then. He had freckles on his nose and sandy hair that kicked up from the front of his cycle helmet. She bet his mother had flattened that every day with a finger full of spit.

'I suggest you leave the hedgehogs alone,' he said, 'and

move along. Don't let me catch you loitering again.' He swung his leg over the bar of the bike.

'You get hedgehogs up in the park by the pond,' he called out, 'near the dinosaurs; I've seen them at dusk when I'm walking the dog…' His voice trailed away into the humming air.

She abandoned her trip to the shops and walked back to her flat. She thought about the greenfinch and wondered how he was doing. How many shots at love did a greenfinch get? He was probably still there, she thought as she buried her chin into her warm jacket, proclaiming his territory.

What had she seen in Ralph? A year ago he'd seemed to offer what she'd wanted: confidence, a career in something he was clear about, and his tweed jackets reminded her of her father. She'd even given him one of her dad's old jackets in the early days, in the flush of love, when his was the only song she could hear in a room full of talented vocalisers. When he'd worn that jacket with its orange flecks and its leather patches, the raw ache of her father's death seemed eased. She'd get it back from him somehow.

In her flat she shivered. There was a chilliness that seemed more than just temperature, there was a lack. Everything seemed lustreless without a promise of love.

She thought of the policeman, and hot shame spread through her body. 'I love nature' – what an idiot! She looked around – the sofa still had the imprint of Ralph's body, her discarded underwear hung at the end of the bed. She threw herself onto the coverlet, smelled him on the sheets. He'd made love to her last night like it had meant something. She picked up her bird book, riffled through its pages.

Despite the apparent deference to the pair bond … most birds remain open to offers throughout the whole breeding season…

She dropped it on the floor. She closed her eyes and thought of Gina's golden throat and satin plumage. She turned over and buried her face in the pillow.

When she woke up the light was fading from the sky. The hours on her own stretched ahead of her. She rolled off the bed and pulled another of her dad's old jackets out of the closet. She pressed it to her face – 'old faithful' he'd called this one – Harris tweed, with capacious pockets that he'd stuffed with sweet chestnuts, acorns and fungi collected during long walks with her through the woods. The checked weave was permeated with pipe-tobacco fumes and the lavender she used to keep away the moths. She shoved her arms into the sleeves and grabbed a belt to cinch the waist.

With the collar around her ears and a scarf around her neck she left the flat and headed for the park. The streetlights had not yet come on though the sky was streaked with orange and the lone walkers with their leashed dogs were already beginning to wander home. The night would soon drift down and cover all this but the traffic queuing up along Anerley Park Road and the occasional laughter from the late walkers made her feel safe.

She took the path around the pond to the side which rose away from the water; in summer that bank would be thick with flowers. Her favourite tree, leafless, but encased in ivy, leaned towards the stone dinosaurs. She stood on the path looking at them over the railings; the bird-beaked, seal-flippered monsters roared soundlessly at the ducks, a frozen remnant of an overactive imagination, a triumph of hope over reality – well she knew all about that. She'd come here with Ralph last summer. She'd sat in his lap in the hollow made by the roots of the leaning tree and told Ralph all about the dinosaurs. She felt a sudden kinship with them, stuck in the mud, pretending to be something they weren't. She poked around in the detritus of the muddy bank. It was damp down here amongst the leaf litter – a perfect place for hungry hedgehogs.

'Found any more mating birds?'

She turned and looked up; the policeman was standing by her favourite tree while a Jack Russell ferreted about at its base.

'I really was looking for hedgehogs, you know,' she called up to him.

'You were behaving suspiciously.'

'I suppose it did look like that.' She dug her toe into the ground, feeling the damp earth give beneath the press of her shoe. 'Well I'd better be going before it gets too dark.'

'Did you find a hedgehog down there?' he said, 'Inspector Gordon there is good at finding hedgehogs.'

'Inspector Gordon?'

'My dog – he's named after a character in Batman.'

The eager dog was sniffing at her shoes. She bent down and scratched the dog's ears.

'He'll be your friend forever if you do that,' he said.

He picked up a ball and tossed it into the dusk – its luminous green shone on the path.

He climbed the few steps down the bank to her, his raised eyebrow an invitation. She walked alongside him in silence.

'So what is it about hedgehogs then?'

She told him her story and he stopped in his tracks.

'Well that is amazing! We had a hedgehog that used to eat cat food too – I'd begun to think I'd made it up. '

'Did you really?' Sally said.

He shook his head, 'No, but I'd like it to be true. I grew up in those flats at the end of Versailles Road – fourth floor – a hedgehog would have needed oxygen to make it up there. Birds were my thing.'

Sally's heart fluttered – a pair of beating wings in the cage of her ribs.

'We had a balcony. One morning near Christmas I found a robin dead on the floor. I was upset so mum bought me some birdseed to help keep the others alive. Progressed from seed to fat balls to peanut feeders – always been ambitious, me,' he smiled, a crescent of promise in the cold night. 'I knew the names of all the birds then, volunteered at the park just so I could see them.'

'I love birds too,' Sally said.

'You're just saying that because you know I want to hear it,' he said.

She shook her head. 'It's true! I've even got blackbirds on my pyjamas.'

They walked round the edge of the pond in silence. The winter moon was a piece of white lichen on the black sky; a fox rippled the long grass and stopped and stared.

'Did you become a policeman just so you could stop innocent girls out bird-watching?'

'No, that's just one of the perks of the job,' he said, 'I get a free bicycle too. Truth is, I come from a copper family, granddad and dad and now me. It's in the genes, never really wanted to be anything else.

They stood still listening for hedgehogs: the warmth of her father's coat wrapped around her body, the air full of night scents, and a feeling that something inside her that she hadn't even realised was asleep, was waking slowly from a long hibernation.

NORWOOD JUNCTION

Recipes for a Successful Working Life
Rosalind Stopps

Duncan knew exactly how many steps there were from his front door to Norwood Junction Station: three hundred and forty three. Three more, just three, and he'd be off the platform and on to the track and *wham* – all over, done and dusted – and he'd never have to think about Big Jim again.

Three hundred and forty six steps, that's all. He counted it out while he practised his baking and he wrote it on flyers for take away pizzas and in the margins of the free newspapers that came through his door. He sang it in his head to the tune of Bohemian Rhapsody, a song his mother used to like, and once, he dialled it on his phone, 346346346, but nobody answered.

In some ways Duncan loved being a working man. He hadn't had many jobs and he wanted to keep this one, he was determined. If he could just learn to deal with his boss Big Jim and stop thinking about the railway line he would be fine. He made up little recipes to keep himself safe.

'A pound of hard work, and a generous sprinkling of good humour,' Duncan thought as he left the flat, toast in hand and ready to face the day. He needed the good humour, for sure. There were days, especially recently, when Big Jim wouldn't leave him alone, as if he had a target drawn on his forehead or a dunce's cap on his head. Anyone would find it hard being the new boy at forty-three years old but it seemed that there were lots of things about work that were difficult to get used to, especially the teasing and jokes. For a change he had a good one up his sleeve today, although he wasn't completely sure if it would go down well. There really ought to be a rule book with bullet points, and Duncan thought that he might write one when he had worked it all out. He would call it 'Recipes for a Successful Working Life' and it would have his name on the cover and a photograph of him looking wise, and possibly bearded. He tried on a wise face as he swallowed the last piece of toast.

The cafe was just to the side of the station, a resting place for weary travellers, a last chance saloon before they struggled home from work. Olive Trees Sandwich Bar, Pizzas and Catering, said the sign, and Duncan felt a surge of pride that almost washed away the anxiety. He wasn't quite sure what an olive tree looked like, but it sounded lovely.

It was a busy place; right on the path from the station and people paid the high prices quite happily just to have the authentic dining experience promised on the menu posted in the window. They had to book some nights or else there were no tables left, that was how popular it was, and he was proud to be part of the team that made it tick.

Let it simmer, he thought as he brushed past the bay trees in the porch and pushed the door open. Let it simmer, whatever happens today, keep the lid on and go back and check it later.

'Hey fuck me, it's Dunkin Donuts,' shouted Big Jim from the kitchen area. Duncan wished that his mother had chosen a different name for him.

'Ignore him,' said Nicky as she bustled past with her arms full of dirty tablecloths, 'he's in a right mood today'.

Duncan smiled at her in a way that he hoped said thank you. Nicky was the best bit about working here, always sunny and never bothered by Big Jim, even when he slapped her bottom or stood too close to her on purpose.

Duncan was ready. 'Hi Jim,' he called out, sticking a smile

on his face like a cherry on a cup cake. He needed to show that he could join in, give as well as take, he thought.

'Been to the gym, Jim?' he said. It was a daring move, and he regretted it as soon as the words were out of his mouth. Big Jim stopped rolling out dough on the counter at the back of the restaurant. It was open plan, the customers liked that but it meant that they had to get as much preparation done as they could before the first diner arrived. Duncan smiled at Big Jim, hoping that he would like the little joke. It had taken him a while to come up with it but he still wasn't sure. Big Jim dusted off his hands very slowly. He brought them together in silent applause but even through the cloud of flour Duncan could see that the smile didn't quite reach Big Jim's eyes.

'Pizza oven needs cleaning,' he said, rubbing his hands together so that the flour cloud puffed down into a smaller, tidier one, as if it had been told to pull itself together smartish.

This was a job that Duncan dreaded. He didn't mind the hard work of it at all, in fact it felt good to get into the warm corners and the nooks and crannies and scrape out the burnt dough and cheesy mess. He knew that good cooks were scrupulously clean, all the books said so, and anyway he liked making a difference, seeing the before and after of it. The problem was Big Jim. Every time Duncan stuck his head in the oven (and he had to, to get it properly clean), Big Jim would think up a new torture. He used to just poke him or 'accidentally' bump into him but recently things had got worse. Once, he had tied Duncan's feet together with string and he hadn't realised until he came back out of the oven and fell off the chair he had been kneeling on. His hip hurt like crazy and Duncan really wanted to cry, but he knew that would make Big Jim even happier so he managed not to until he got home that night.

Another time, and even worse, Big Jim got the broom and put it suggestively by Duncan's bottom. 'Having fun?' he called out and Duncan, not knowing the broom was there, said, 'yes thanks, I really like it.' He didn't hear the sniggers because apart from being in the oven, his head was full of other stuff, like which pie he might bake that evening when he got home, and whether melted cheese could be used as glue in a tight spot. In fact, he would never have known if Big Jim hadn't insisted on telling him.

'Ooh look, your favourite broom,' he always said now when Duncan was sweeping, and sometimes he grabbed it and pretended to dance and kiss.

Duncan wondered what would happen this time.

He didn't have to wait long. As he knelt on the chair and reached inside the oven with a scraping knife he could definitely hear Big Jim giggling, and something wet slapped on to the back of his legs. He tried to work out what to do, but he could only see two choices. Keep quiet, take it on the chin and keep the job, or walk out with dignity, go back on benefits and say goodbye to Nicky; no-one would care. The oven would probably never get cleaned properly again, he knew that no-one could do it like he could. All the dirt and nasty bits would be burnt to a charcoal layer that smoked whenever it was lit. No, he had to stay.

'The perfect dish requires patience,' he thought. 'Maybe if I wait it out he'll get tired, or realise how upset I am and stop.'

The heavy, wet feeling was getting stronger and even inside the oven Duncan could smell fish. He scraped a little more but his heart wasn't in it, so he pulled his head out and twisted round with a sense of dread. He was right to feel worried. Big Jim was bent over with laughter and across the backs of his legs, pinning him in place, was a huge fish, wet from the bucket Big Jim was holding. It was a horror film fish, mouth open and teeth bared. He knew that it must be dead, but Duncan screamed anyway, he couldn't help it.

He gripped the knife in both hands. Duncan didn't want to get into trouble; he didn't want that at all. He just wanted to clean the oven and mop the floor and do all the other jobs that he was so good at, but he really didn't like that fish at all, not one bit, and he certainly didn't want to touch it.

'Woohoo,' said Big Jim, 'are you threatening me, Dunkin Donuts?' He stopped laughing as if someone had flicked a switch.

'Could you move the fish?' Duncan said.

'That's a bit rude,' said Big Jim, 'I think you should say please.'

All the laughter had gone from his face. The glitter in his eye came from something else completely, a hatred Duncan had seen before but couldn't understand. He didn't mind saying please, of course he didn't, but with a creeping misery Duncan realised that it wouldn't be enough. If he said please, there would be something else Big Jim wanted him to do, today, tomorrow and every day until he got another job, which might take years.

'Could you just move the fish?' he said, keeping his voice as steady as he could.

Big Jim looked furious. Duncan thought that it was a little like making pastry – what was needed was a steady hand and an ability to keep a cool head even when it was all going wrong. He was good on theory even though his pastry was always tough and chewy.

'Pretty please, Big Jim,' said Big Jim in a quieter, more threatening voice.

'That's it,' said Nicky, dropping a handful of knives and forks into the sink in the corner, 'I've had enough, and I don't care if you sack me, Jim. Take the goddamn fish off him and let's get back to work. You really are an arse sometimes.'

'It was a joke,' Big Jim said in a voice that sounded anything but funny.

'I don't think so,' said Nicky, 'no-one is laughing.'

'You have no sense of humour,' said Big Jim.

'I said that's enough, and I meant it. Do you reckon you could find someone else to work in this shithole for the wages you pay us?'

Big Jim kept his indignant glare going a second longer then slopped the fish back into the bucket and pretended to smile. Duncan thought that it might be safe to join in while he still had the knife in his hand.

'I don't think it's funny either,' he said, getting off the chair and trying to brush down the back of his trousers without slashing them.

'Oh, fuck the lot of you,' Big Jim said, 'none of you knows what a joke is.' He stormed off towards his office, leaving a trail of fishy drips as the bucket swung backwards and forwards in his hand.

'Re-fucking-sult,' said Nicky, holding her thumb up to Duncan.

'Re-fucking-sult,' Duncan repeated, although he didn't usually like to swear. 'Sometimes a tricky dish that isn't working can be rescued by an unusual ingredient.' He'd read that in one of his cookbooks but hadn't ever realised what it could mean.

'Whatever,' said Nicky.

Duncan clambered back into the oven with a smile. He might make some cakes tonight, he thought, and bring them in tomorrow for the team.

WEST CROYDON

All Roads Begin at West Croydon
Max Hawker

February

The sun throws its pint-of-blood spill over Croydon's townscape.

In a quiet, concrete neighbourhood, Rishwan Kabi pulls up to the curb in his X-reg. Vauxhall. He looks past excuses for gardens at several terraced houses, slack in the murk of dawn. He pulls out his mobile and rings a number.

Brr brr. Brr brr. 'Hello, yes, madam. Yes, your cab is outside. Okay.'

Rishwan turns the radio down a little. He's had enough of NonStopPlay. He opens his wallet and half pulls out a photo. Three faces look back at him. One big. Two small.

Just five more months, Kali, he thinks, *why did you make me come here, my jaan? All I wanted was to be with you. But you...*

The rear passenger door opens and a large, middle-aged black woman struggles in with a huge bag. She is a cyclone of yellows, reds and greens. She sucks her teeth when the door swings into her elbow.

'Good morning, madam. Where are you going?'

'West Croydon Station.'

No need for the sat nav this time. Indicator. Check – clear. Accelerate.

The hills and roads scroll away. The occasional guzzle of static-meets-human-voice comes from the aged Kirisun.

Rishwan doesn't mind the silence, but his client's thick, chesty breath is distracting him. He decides that if she's talking, her breathing won't be so noticeable.

'Going anywhere nice?'

'What you say?'

'I said: going anywhere nice?'

'Yes. Going home.'

'Been away long?'

'Not seen Jamaica in maybe three year.'

'Three year? Long time. I've been over here exactly twenty-six months and five days.'

Minutes decay. Silence. Silence. Silence – except for thick, chesty breath. Rishwan decides to give it another go, but as he makes to speak, his client's mobile rings.

'Yeah, hello. In the cab, going to the station. What you talking about? Flight delayed? How long? You phoned Alice? Yeah, I think you should. Don't go crying on me. We'll make it. No, there's no duppy after you. Mm-hmm. Yep. Bye.'

Several minutes later, Rishwan hears a wet snivel accompanying the continuing chesty breath. He glances at the mirror to find his client crying.

'Are you okay?'

'Umm, yes, yes.'

'Flights get delayed all the time. Don't worry. I remember when I first –'

'Yes, but I didn't need this flight to be delayed. You see, I'm going home 'cos it's my brother's funeral –'

'I'm sorry,' Rishwan auto-replies.

'– and it's tomorrow morning. But the flight's delayed near half a day. Yolande's already checked in so I'll have to go meet her. She's in a state.'

I remember baba's funeral on the Ganges, Rishwan recalls, *windy day and the bloody flame blew out. Took half an hour to bring his boat back in again.*

'Three years since you seen Jamaica, you say? Did your brother come over at all?'

The cab comes to a stop at traffic lights.

'Not once. Trevor weren't the type to travel. He was a stubborn fool. Right through to the last.'

'The last?'

Amber – Green. Accelerate.

'That's right. Trevor was a fireman, see. Well respected in the community, you know? Helped put out the big fire of '97 at the old Lawrence house. He had a burn like a cross on his cheek – Jesus was always watching him. Trevor, he were good at what he did, and the town loved him for it, but he was such a heavy drinker. Played poker with the boys over several bottles of rum – would do that week in, week out. An' when he drink, he get all zealous with the ladies and be urinating in the street, jus' like one of them good-for-nothing youths over here. People would say: 'You may be a good fireman, but you ain't anywhere near good enough to put out the fire in the hereafter, if you keep up this way'. Anyway, 'bout seven day ago, Trevor be on the beach, in naught but the skin God gave him, and he dancin' under a coconut tree. Then bop! He knocked on the head by a falling coconut. Stone dead. Poor fool.'

Rishwan turns the car on to London Road, less than a minute from the station.

'Least he didn't suffer, eh?'

The passenger sighs. 'Aye. Least he didn't suffer. But now he gone selfishly make me go through a long flight there and back again. Did he think about my suffering when he was dancing under them coconuts? Lots of travel. I can't be doing that.'

'You have a chance to make your peace with him though.'

Silence returns for a few seconds more. Rishwan notices a change come over his client's face.

'Aye. Maybe you're right. Maybe you're right. 'Strive for peace with all, and for the holiness without which you won't see the Lord'.'

Rishwan brings the car to a stop, twenty-five yards from the station.

'Seven pounds please.'

The client hands Rishwan the money. 'Thank you, and take care now, young man.' The door slams.

Rishwan watches the black woman move off up the road. He looks around the car, then opens his wallet and half pulls out a photo. Three faces look back at him. One big. Two small.

Kali, you left me here, all alone, Rishwan sighs, *how could you?*

*

March

Rishwan checks his mirror, indicates, and turns right. Friday night revellers clutter the streets. He quickly glances up again. The rear-view mirror is a canvas upon which two teenagers kiss. Rishwan tries to ignore the light squelches coming from fused lips.

'Yer so hot – I cou' fu' you righ' now.'

'We'll be at mine soon. Just hold on a bit longer. Stop that. What are you like?'

I remember that age, Rishwan reflects, *and Kali dressed in that sari. She was so beautiful.*

'How many stops 's it from Wes' Croy'on, babe?'

'Three. Pull that back down! Why don't you tell me what you're going to do to me, Chris?'

We'd make love in the garden of the big manor house, Rishwan smiles, *and get chased off by the gardener in the morning.*

'Baby, I'm gonna run my han' righ' down yer body to yer toes –'

The girl giggles.

'– Then I'm gonna run my han' righ' ba' up 'gain.'

You told me how you wanted to move on from India and see the world, Rishwan remembers, *and that, as long as we had each other, there was something to live for.*

'I'll tear open yer dress an' ta' yer tits in my mouth...'

'Chris – I want that so bad.'

We came here – and then you were pregnant, and all your dreams were broken when the twins were born. Why was it my fault though?

'Then I'll squeeze yer thighs, an' move up ter yer hot, wet – Eurgh, I don' feel so goo'.'

'Chris?'

'I think I'm gonna be sick!'

'You bastard! It's all over my lap! You stupid prick!'

'Oh thanks, who gonna clean that up, eh?' Rishwan snaps, reasserting his place in reality.

*

April

'Awright? Can ya take us to West Croydon, mate?'

'Yes. Please get in.'

Three large white men roll into the back seat, each stinking of booze. Rishwan decides he does not want any kind of conversation with them, not that he expects to get any, and so turns Radio 5 Live up.

'Yeah, so that's why yer fucked when Juan leaves. Both yer strikers and yer wingers need Juan behind 'em to play their best.'

'He might not go.'

Two of the three men jeer.

From the radio comes football punditry, something Rishwan has never fully understood the need for. He's never had much time for football, but many of his passengers have been keen to talk about the sport. Rishwan's solution is to pick up as much as he can on the radio, and routinely change who he supports to whichever team is unlikely to upset X, Y or Z passenger.

You hated that about this country straight away, Rishwan

thinks, *the Neanderthals on weekends drunk and chanting outside pubs. The world wasn't what you'd hoped it would be, was it, Kali?*

'Oi, I'm talkin' ter ya.'

Rishwan feels a tug at his shoulder. 'Yes! Yes? Sorry, sir. …Yes?'

'I said: 'oo d'ya suppor'?'

Shit, he panics; *I didn't hear who they support. Play it safe. No gambles. No Arsenals or Tottenhams or Millwalls.*

'Me? I'm a – Dagenham & Redbridge man.'

The three men laugh.

'What d'ya think abou' Albert Juan handin' in 'is transfer request?'

Rishwan muses, Albert Juan… Think. Think. He – plays for –Arsenal!

'– He'll be missed. But as long as he doesn't go to a local rival then that's alright, eh?'

'Whatchoo talkin' 'bout? The stupid Spanish cun' is *'omesick* – he ent lookin' to move across London. An' 'e jus' 'appens ter be 'omesick when Real come sniffin'. Fuckin' funny coincidence, tha'!'

Homesick. I remember home, Rishwan thinks. *Cumin drifting up the hill. Mad Dev on the corner. That three-legged dog the kids played cricket with. Mr Juan, I know your pain.*

'Whatchoo think, boss?' One of the men is addressing Rishwan. 'It possible ter play two seasons over 'ere and suddenly get 'omesick?'

Rishwan considers the question. 'I don't know. Possibly, yes. Maybe you go to a new country and you have all these ideas and you try to make it work out, but it doesn't. Maybe you know you have a duty over in this new country, but your heart is elsewhere. Maybe this Juan is looking at the end of his contract and can't wait to go, whether Real come in for him or not.'

How many more conversations about football until I see you again, Kali? Did you ever consider how hard it would be for me? I knew what needed to be done. It still hurt though.

*

May

Rishwan hasn't been this far out of his usual driving route before. He taps West Croydon Station into his sat nav, just in case he loses his bearing. The Kirisun scratches the car's silence, and Rishwan answers. 'Outside the house, just waiting for him to come down.'

Less than two months now, Kali. What do our babies look like? Can they say any words yet? I wonder how heavy they'll be in my arms, Rishwan smiles. *And you – will you be the same woman who told me that we couldn't raise our children over here – that they needed to be in their proper culture? Will you be the same woman who told me to stay here and earn, that no job in India would do to pay for us all? Do I want to see you again, and see that you haven't changed?*

The passenger seat opens and a thin man hops in, clasping a small holdall.

'Good morning. West Croydon Station, please.'

Indicator. Check – clear. Accelerate.

Rishwan notices his passenger take off a wedding ring and place it on the dashboard.

'Eight years,' he sighs. 'Can't believe I'm doing this.'

Rishwan keeps quiet.

'This is one of those days, my friend. One of those rare days when we make a decision that will affect our lives forever.'

'That so?'

'Yep. That is so. I've just left my wife and daughter. I've had enough and I'm off.'

Rishwan isn't sure how to respond, at first. 'Why?'

'Why? Because I can. I work my balls off day in, day out. And all I'm doing is fuelling them, as though it's their God-given right. And what do I get? Four hours of crap telly every night and sex once a week. Nah, that's not me anymore. I'm gonna get on that train, go to the airport, and throw myself out into the world and just see what happens. Leave it all to chance, to chaos. Scares the hell out of me, but that's good. It means I care.'

We not only shared that dream, Kali, we built it up together. We were there, on the brink of tossing ourselves to the elements. What kind of life was there ready for us?

Rishwan has never had a passenger like this before. Occasionally someone comes along who is keen to chat, but they never say anything overly personal.

'Don't you care what happens to them?' Rishwan finally asks.

'Course I do. I've left them with enough to keep them going for a while. It simply means my wife will have to get off of her arse and work now. Or she'll have to make the effort of moving on and finding someone else. At the end of the day, this is my life, and I only get one chance to make myself happy. I expect millions of people around the world want to do the same. Well, there's nothing stopping any of them doing what I'm doing. I don't feel ashamed for taking that chance.'

Rishwan overtakes a bus.

'Why are you telling me any of this?'

'Well, you're the first person I've seen since leaving them, and I want to hear what you think.'

'I'm not paid to judge.'

Maybe he's right, Rishwan wonders, *what is there holding any of us back from making ourselves happy?*

There is no further conversation.

*

June

The entrance to West Croydon Station stands before Rishwan, a cave winding back into an unknown. He must have dropped scores of people off here over the months, but he has never, himself, been inside.

Today is the day of days. The flight from Heathrow out to

Delhi is booked. The trains up into London are regular enough.

We came here, Kali, we came here thinking it would be the first port on a long voyage. My god, that was less than three years ago. And now it's almost eighteen months since I saw you. Not even a thank you for the money I send you, no letter to tell me how you all are. All of you – lost over there in a bubble of memory. And here I am at a junction to the future.

He grips his light suitcase a little tighter, and the surrounding people seem to fade into the background.

What happens when I find you? Can things ever be normal? Can we ever be happy? How far can that future we want stretch on for? What is there to discover, learn, do? I know what must be done...

He opens his wallet and half pulls out a photo. Three faces look back at him. One big. Two small.

ABOUT ARACHNE PRESS

Arachne Press is primarily a publisher of fiction, particularly short fiction. We aim to showcase new and established writers in a series of collaborations with Liars' League and in other unconnected anthologies and collections. We will also publish poetry, novels, fiction for children and selected non-fiction.

BOOKS

Stations is our second book.

Our first book, *London Lies*, ISBN: 978-1-909208-00-1 was our first Liars' League showcase. Featuring short stories from nineteen authors who have been showcased at London's Liars' League, the monthly live literature event.

Moving from 1930s Camden to a Royal Wedding 'riot', via football fights, office steeplechases and awkward dates in art galleries, *London Lies* is a bizarre, funny, moving and sometimes unnerving glimpse into the secret life of the city we all love and know – or do we?

Our next book is due out in late January 2013 and will be a valentine's day anthology, in collaboration with Liars' League, with a provisional title of Lovers' Lies.

EVENTS

Arachne Press is enthusiastic about live literature and makes an effort to present our books through readings. If you run a bookshop, a literature festival or any other kind of literature venue, get in touch, we'd love to talk to you.

WORKSHOPS

Arachne Press offers writing workshops, available as one-off or a series of linked events, suitable for writers groups, literature festivals, evening classes – if you are interested, please get in touch.

INFORMATION FOR WRITERS

Arachne Press will start considering unsolicited submissions from April 2013.

We are most interested in collections of short stories, but will consider novels, whether literary or genre, with the exception of erotica and horror.

we will also consider poetry and fiction aimed at children and young adults.

Please look at our submission guidelines on our website.

www.arachnepress.com